BARTHOLOMÄUS ZIEGENBALG

The Estate of The Clergy Pleasing to God

AN ABRIDGED SELECTION OF HIS BOOK WRITTEN IN PRISON

BARTHOLOMÄUS ZIEGENBALG

THE ESTATE OF THE CLERGY PLEASING TO GOD
AN ABRIDGED SELECTION OF HIS BOOK WRITTEN IN PRISON

Edited on behalf of the Francke Foundations by

Niels-Peter Moritzen

Translated by

Rekha Vaidya Rajan

2019

Bartholomäus Ziegenbalg: *The Estate of The Clergy Pleasing to God - An abridged selection of his book written in prison* - Published by the Rev. Dr. Ashish Amos of the Indian Society for Promoting Christian Knowledge (ISPCK), Post Box 1585, Kashmere Gate, Delhi-110006.

ISBN: 978-93-88945-39-4

Laser typeset by

ISPCK, Post Box 1585, 1654, Madarsa Road, Kashmere Gate, Delhi-110006 • *Tel:* 23866323

e-mail: ashish@ispck.org.in • ella@ispck.org.in
website: www.ispck.org.in

Contents

FOREWORD

In 2006 the first Protestant mission in the history of the Church celebrates its tercentenary jubilee. Its founder is Bartholomäus Ziegenbalg who, along with his colleague Heinrich Plütschau, received the mandate from the Danish king, Frederick IV in 1705 to set up an Evangelical-Lutheran mission in the small Danish trading colony Tranquebar on the south-east coast of India. On July 9, 1706 the two theologians reached their destination and immediately began their work. From this there arose a flourishing mission enterprise in South India which August Hermann Francke's orphan-house in Halle directed organizationally and logistically, which it supported materially and with personnel, and guided intellectually and spiritually. As the first missionary of the Danish Halle mission Bartholomäus Ziegenbalg is still highly respected all over the world in the Evangelical-Lutheran Church.

In the year 2006 an international jubilee programme will commemorate the establishment of the Danish-Halle mission, which also constituted the opening phase of a peaceful cultural dialogue between Europe and India that continues till today. This is also evident in the joint preparation and execution of the jubilee programme by the Francke Foundations and its Indian partners, especially the Gurukul Lutheran Theological College and Research Institute in Chennai. In the framework of this joint jubilee programme many new publications on the history of the Danish-Halle mission will also appear. This publication here belongs to Ziegenbalg's so-called prison texts. It is not meant to be a scientific edition of the sources. Rather, it wishes to allow Ziegenbalg himself to speak, as the editor Niels-Peter Moritzen emphasizes. A special thanks goes to him for the fact that this manuscript of Ziegenbalg has been brought to light here in the publishing house of the Francke Foundations 296 years after he had written it in the fortress Dansborg in Tranquebar and sent to Halle to be published. Over the centuries the manuscript was carefully preserved in the archives of the Foundation. Today it is to be found in the main archives under the catalogue number AFSt/H B 75 and B 76. A few years after the Francke Foundations were re-established in 1992 Mrs. Ulla Sandgren from Uppsala approached me with the request to publish her hand-written transcription of this Ziegenbalg manuscript. I am very happy that we can now fulfill her justified wish thanks to the conscientious work of re-editing done by Prof. Emeritus Moritzen. This text-edition is not aimed primarily at academics of any specific branch of science but at a general public that is interested in reading Ziegenbalg in the original. The rules governing this edition, as explained by the editor in his introduction, are, therefore, also oriented towards this group of readers.

Ziegenbalg's book about the estate of the clergy pleasing to God is the moving testament of a deeply pious man who was stirred by the spirit of Halle-Pietism and who strove to carry his Christian beliefs out into the world. He serves even today as a shining example of the ability to encounter other cultures and religions with interest and respect, while at the same time, maintaining one's own firm beliefs. Ziegenbalg shows us that this is not a contradiction, but rather a condition for such encounters.

Halle, October 2005

Dr. Thomas Müller-Bahlke
Director of the Francke Foundations

EDITOR'S INTRODUCTION

After working for two years in Tranquebar, South India, the Royal Danish Missionary, Bartholomäus Ziegenbalg was imprisoned from 19.11.1708 till 26.3.1709 in Fort Dansborg on the orders of the Danish city commandant Johan Sigismund Hassius. In contemporary terms it would be called preventive custody. He was released without any charges being brought against him.

What does a missionary do in prison? He would have liked to continue working on the translation of the Bible into Tamil, but he was prevented from doing that. He sings and prays, and some of the guards who sympathize with him do the same to cheer him up. He meditates, and when, after a month, a soldier secretly brings him paper and a white lead quill at night he sets his meditation down on paper (Lehmann 111). He writes almost a thousand pages, more than seven hundred about "An Estate of The Clergy Pleasing to God" and a shorter text about "A Christianity Pleasing to God".

Why was Ziegenbalg imprisoned? He explains it to his readers in a preface which is also given here, but which was only written when he sent the manuscripts to Germany with his helpful writer Christian Ludwig.

The latest study on this question (Nörgaard 1988) comes to the following conclusion: "I do not think it is possible to lay the blame entirely either on Hassius or on Ziegenbalg. The fault—or the reason—was the simple but serious fact that the two things: commercial interests and mission, were incompatible and that, despite this, if both sides wanted to work alongside one another, they would have to give up some of their principles." (47)

Today one often hears that there was no deep contradiction, but rather a close cooperation between colonialism and mission. Here we have before us a severe conflict in early times. The tiny Danish colony paid an annual rent to the ruler of Tanjore and did not represent a threat to Indian culture.

The commandant, Hassius, was employed by the trading company and was accountable to it. The missionaries had been sent out directly by the king, and the working relations between both had not been clarified.

In the Danish colony it was customary to employ Portuguese-speaking Catholic Indians. Almost none of the Europeans could speak a local language—except Ziegenbalg. He gained the trust of some Europeans, especially among the soldiers, many of who spoke German, and he also gained access to the local population. He stood up for the disadvantaged baptismal aspirants and members of the congregation and demanded space and rights for the evangelical congregation that was being formed among the local population.

Those who wish to know more about this will find—apart from the introduction—only a few dozen places where Ziegenbalg talks about his work and his experiences. Together they constitute less than eight pages, but all of them are contained in this selection.

The manuscript has been carefully preserved till now, but it has not been published and hardly used. In 2006 there will be a commemoration in India and Europe of the beginning of the evangelical mission 300 years ago. And, what is being presented here, namely a strongly abridged selection, is part of this jubilee.

In an accompanying letter of 30.8.1709 to Joachim Lange, a professor of theology in Halle (Lehmann 539), Ziegenbalg explains that a fair copy of his manuscript was made by a helper, that he had also hurriedly gone through it, but that there were sure to be some mistakes. Before publishing it, it should be proof-read. This has now happened in such a way that we would like to expect the reader to follow Ziegenbalg's language in a largely unchanged form. In the orthography however, we have adapted the words and punctuation generally to the rules of contemporary orthography. In addition, we have reduced the Latin elements: Latin endings in the names of people and places have been left out and some expressions have been changed into German. The Latin expressions that have remained, but also other difficult words, are explained in brackets. In a few places difficult words in quotations from the Bible have been replaced with corresponding words from a later revision of the Bible. Because, our aim is not so much to produce the correct edition of a historical document, but rather to let Ziegenbalg speak for himself.

The book is dedicated to teachers, preachers and students of theology in Germany and Denmark, "for the edification of my faithful teachers and those of others, and also in order to use my talents for the welfare of my fellow-men even while in prison".

Why was the text not published at that time? We can only fall back on conjecture. First, the text is voluminous. Then there is the fact that it not suitable either as information or for publicity and, therefore, provides hardly any material for a historian today.

Finally, there was public opinion which was very critical of Halle-Pietism and the mission.

There is also the fact that on 15.10.1714 a mutual amnesty was agreed upon in Tranquebar between Hassius and Ziegenbalg, "that the hitherto existing disputes [...] should be forgotten, forgiven and should forever be ended on the basis of this written agreement between us" (HB 647-649).

This agreement was published in Halle and about Ziegenbalg's stay in prison it was only mentioned that it had come to an end. After this amnesty one could no longer publish the preface to the text.

Today we read the text primarily as the testament of a missionary in prison and how he deals with his tribulations. He is also aware of the fact "that he has used many and extensive parts of the Bible in it"—almost 1800, and often many verses following one after the other—but, "this happened because I could find far greater comfort in them than in my own words".

Thus: the meditations of a persecuted missionary needing comfort, written with a white lead quill in prison with no aids other than the Holy Scriptures.

His method of working can be reconstructed: He meditates on his theme and develops sub-divisions. In this way a well-planned structure emerges with no less than nine large parts with 70 chapters overall. In this abridged selection the structure has been reproduced in its entirety.

Then, in a second step, he begins to fill this structure and here, the Holy Bible plays the main role. Ziegenbalg's Bible also contains the apocrypha which he uses extensively. The Luther-translation of his time deviates in its language and sometimes also in verse numbers from what is common today. Generally, Ziegenbalg mentions the exact chapter and verse numbers of his Bible quotations, but he makes the text a part of his own train of thoughts and there are explanatory additions. It cannot have escaped him completely that there are numerous overlaps and repetitions, but he does not let that bother him.

Ziegenbalg was, at that time, 26 years old, unmarried, and did not have many years of experience in the ministry. This may have contributed to the fact that his portrayal of the estate of the clergy pleasing to God is marked by such a strong contrast. He can portray the estate of the clergy pleasing to God most clearly from the Holy Scriptures, while the daily reality of the Church presents him mainly with numerous counter-examples. Here there are the unconverted teachers and hirelings who speak to please men, who look for recognition and honour and for whom the job of the clergyman is only a means of earning a livelihood—a strangely gloomy framework.

The portrayal is, however, marked by the basic belief that Pietism voices particularly strongly: One who has not comprehended Christianity with his heart, for whom it has not become a lived experience, such a person might be able to talk correctly about it, but he cannot convince, cannot win people over. In questions of dogma Ziegenbalg did not deviate from the Lutheran catechism. But, disputes about dogma are not his passion.

I would like to briefly point out two special beliefs: Ziegenbalg is of the opinion that a properly converted teacher who is touched by the Holy Spirit becomes a wellspring so that he does not have to work out each sermon in advance thoroughly and painstakingly as a teacher does who has understood the gospel only with his head. Once his notes have come to an end, he does not know what to say. How different is the one touched by the Holy Spirit!

This also reflects Ziegenbalg's own experience and talent, but the editor would not consider this ability as a definite sign of an endowment by the Spirit.

The other belief is that a teacher pleasing to God should not make any attempts to get a ministry, but he should allow the inner and outer vocation to ripen, which means that he should wait till he is called. That is how Ziegenbalg did it himself.

It now remains to explain the aspects determining the selection. There is the structure which provides an overview over the whole text. There are parts 1 and 2—abridged, especially long quotations from the Bible, and there are the paragraphs in which Ziegenbalg gives some idea of the situation in Tranquebar. There is chapter 1 of part 9 which gives us a good insight into the use of the Scriptures. And, naturally, the introduction at the beginning which Ziegenbalg wrote shortly before sending the manuscript to Europe. Wherever it has been abridged it is a question of entire parts, chapters or paragraphs.

We are publishing this abridged edition in the hope that Ziegenbalg himself can be heard in it and can move the hearts of the readers. The entire text is available in the archives of the Francke Foundations under the catalogue number AFSt/E 2005.35.

Niels-Peter Moritzen

Literature:

HB = Hallesche Berichte: Der Königlich Dänischen Missionarien aus Ost-Indien eingesandte ausführliche Berichte. Halle 1710 ff.

Arno Lehmann: Alte Briefe aus Indien. Unveröffentlichte Briefe von Bartholomäus Ziegenbalg 1706-1719. Berlin 1957.

Anders Nörgaard: Mission und Obrigkeit. Die dänisch-hallische Mission in Tranquebar 1706-1845. Gütersloh 1988.

On the Source,
Its History and the Abridged Selection

Based on the manuscript written by Ziegenbalg in prison with a white lead quill, made into a fair copy by Christian Ludwig, soldier in Tranquebar and honorary sacristan, and brought to Europe.

Transcribed from his manuscript, preserved in the archives of the Francke Foundations, and copied in fair with suggestions for corrections by Mrs. Ulla Sandgren in Uppsala, former missionary in South India. Based on Ulla Sandgren's manuscript, written in the computer by Mrs. Hildegard Wickert, publishing assistant in Erlangen. Introduced, corrected and abridged by Prof. Emeritus Niels-Peter Moritzen in Erlangen.

Translator's Note

The translation of this text by Ziegenbalg would not have been possible without the active help of Dr. Erika Pabst who provided answers and solutions to my questions and who read through the drafts with a vigilant eye. The mistakes that remain are my own.

Ziegenbalg writes long and structurally complicated sentences that had to be often broken up into smaller sentences while translating them, while maintaining the meaning that he wishes to convey.

Rendering the Bible passages into English cannot be the work of a translator today since there are many accepted English versions of the Bible. The question remained about which version should be used. Initially, the idea was to use the King James Bible, since it was closest in time to Ziegenbalg's text. However, the English used here is antiquated and might have presented problems for the readers. The decision to use the New International Version (NIV) rested not only on the fact that it is a translation into contemporary English, but that it is one of the most widely read English Bible translations besides the King James Bible. While its language is modern, its theological direction is said to be Protestant-conservative.

However, there are certain passages in Ziegenbalg's text that are not to be found in the New International Version or in any other Protestant Bible. These are mainly the so-called "Wisdom Chapters", for which an English version of the Catholic Bible has been used. The source for these passages has been provided in a footnote. One quote from Sirach is only available in the website mentioned in the footnote. All other passages are taken from the New International Version provided in the website http://www.biblegateway.com.

At some places, the verse numbers provided by Ziegenbalg diverge from the verse numbers in the New International Version. In such cases the number in the NIV has been given. These are as follows:

- Part II, Chapter 2, § 1. Ecclesiastes 7:11, not 7.12 as mentioned by Ziegenbalg.

- Part II, Chapter 2, § 23. Wisdom 9 has only 18 verses according to the source used, not 19 as mentioned by Ziegenbalg. However, the cited passage is contained in the verses till 18.

- Part II, Chapter 3, § 10. Ziegenbalg mentions John 5:39. The passage cited includes verse 40 from the NIV.

- Part II, Chapter 3, § 17. Ziegenbalg mentions Psalm 19:8,9. The passage quoted is contained in the verses 7-9.

- Part II, Chapter 3, § 17. Ziegenbalg mentions Sirach 24:34-37. In the source used the cited passage is contained in the verses 25-27.

- Part II, Chapter 4, § 19. In the Bible passage marked Exodus 4:15, Ziegenbalg only quotes the second part of the verse.

- Part II, Chapter 4, § 19. In the passage quoted marked Romans 15:18 Ziegenbalg only uses the first part of the verse.

- Part II, Chapter 6, § 9. In the passage marked Romans 5:3,4 Ziegenbalg only quotes part of the verses.

- Part IX, Chapter 1, § 11. Ziegenbalg quotes from Maleachi 2:7. However, the last sentence, "ein Engel des Herrn Zebaoth" does not appear in the NIV. (Presumably, Ziegenbalg had the Stade-Bible of 1703 with him, which also formed the textual basis for the Canstein-Bible. See: Biblia: Das ist: Die gantze Heil. Schrifft Altes und Neues Testaments...) The translation is, therefore, mine.

I would like to thank the Francke Foundations for entrusting the task of translation to me and I would particularly like to thank Dr. Erika Pabst for her help and support.

Rekha Vaidya Rajan

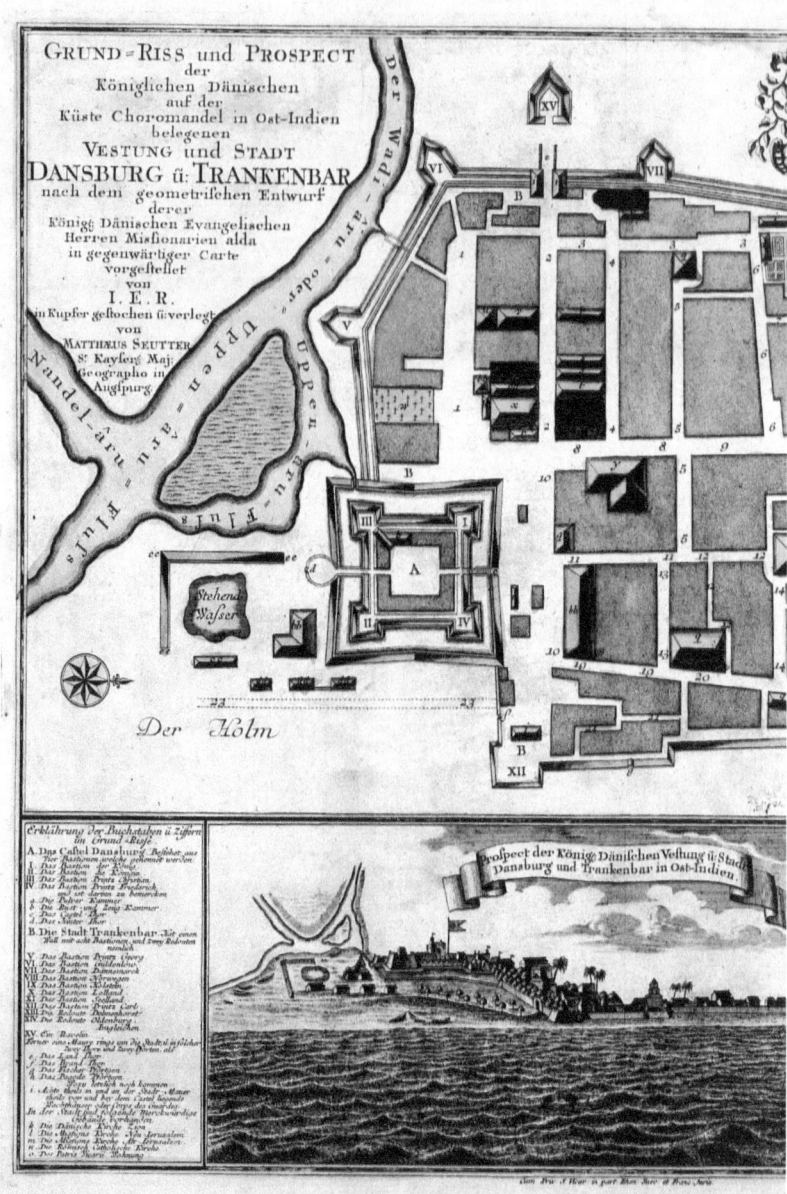

GRUND=RISS und PROSPECT
der
Königlichen Dänischen
auf der
Küste Choromandel in Ost-Indien
belegenen
VESTUNG und STADT
DANSBURG ü: TRANKENBAR
nach dem geometrischen Entwurf
derer
Königl: Dänischen Evangelischen
Herren Missionarien alda
in gegenwärtiger Carte
vorgestellet
von
I. E. R.
in Kupfer gestochen ü: verlegt
von
MATTHÆUS SEUTTER
Sr: Kayserl: Maj:
Geographo in
Augspurg

Der Wadi = aru oder Uppen = aru = Fluss

Nandel = aru = Fluss

Stehend Wasser

Der Holm

Erklährung der Buchstaben ü: Ziffern
im Grund=Risse

A. Das Cabel Dansburg Besthet aus
    Vier Bastionen welche genennet werden.
I. Das Bastion der König:
II. Das Bastion de Königin
III. Das Bastion Printz Christian
IV. Das Bastion Printz Friderich
    und ist daran zu bemerken.
1. Die Pulver=Kammer
2. Die Burst: und Zeug Kammer
3. Das Capell=Thor
4. Das Water=Thor

B. Die Stadt Trankenbar hat einen
    Wall mit acht Bastionen und Zwey Redouten
    nemlich.
V. Das Bastion Printz Georg
VI. Das Bastion Dannemarck
VII. Das Bastion Dannemarck
VIII. Das Bastion Norwegen
IX. Das Bastion Holstein
X. Das Bastion Lolland
XI. Das Bastion Gotland
XII. Das Bastion Printz Carl
XIII. Die Redoute Dannschwerd
XV. Ein Bastion Oldenburg
XV. Ein Bastion

Prospect der König: Dänischen Vestung ü: Stadt
Dansburg und Trankenbar in Ost-Indien.

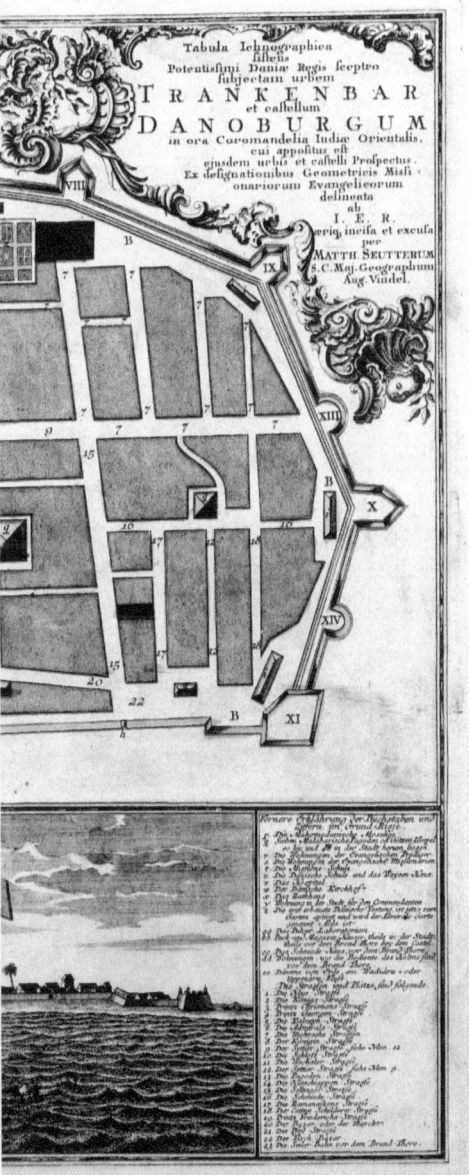

Plan and View of Fort Dansborg and the city of Tranquebar, coloured copperplate engraving by Matthäus Seuter based on the drawing done by a missionary in Tranquebar, Augsburg, around 1745, 52×60 cm. (Germany, Francke Foundations: BFSt: Kt: 256)

BARTHOLOMÄUS ZIEGENBALG

The Estate of The Clergy Pleasing to God
AN ABRIDGED SELECTION OF HIS BOOK WRITTEN IN PRISON

Dedication of Ziegenbalg's Book

All
faithful teachers and
witnesses of the truth
in
Denmark and Germany
but especially
to those dearly beloved
and esteemed Fathers in the Lord
in both royal residences
Copenhagen and Berlin
as also in the Friedrichs University
of Halle
who have hitherto, through prayer, advice and deeds
shown great care in promoting God's work among the heathens
and will continue to do so in the future.
Wishing
divine help for the blessed administration of their holy
ministries and the spirit of heavenly wisdom for propagating
the merciful kingdom of Jesus Christ, along with all the
beneficial well-being of body and soul,
here in time and there in eternity.
Amen!

ZIEGENBALG'S PREFACE TO HIS BOOK

Highly Venerable
dearly beloved Fathers in Christ Jesus,
highly esteemed Friends and Patrons.

It has pleased the gracious God to send me from our beloved
Europe here to East India among the heathens in order to see
whether the Christian doctrine can be planted here among these
blind peoples. Having worked here for more than three years in
my ministry and, with God's grace, having learnt their language,
I have found a good response from them so that, both verbally
and in writing, the name of the living God and of our Lord and
Saviour Jesus Christ could be proclaimed to them for their
salvation. I, therefore, praise the uncommon kindness of God
that I have experienced in this work and wish that all pious
theologians may praise and glorify God fervently for such blessing
and help. At the same time, however, I must lament with a
melancholy heart that many heathens in this place have been
hindered in their conversion by the European Christians here,
partly because of their vexatious lifestyle, but partly also because
of those un-Christian procedures that have been used against me
and my colleague. Because those people who should have promoted
this holy work in every way and should have found special joy

and happiness in it, they have instead opposed it the most and have thought of all means through which the work could be hindered and stopped. And, because our conscience compelled us to show them their un-Christian ways, they finally put me in prison, although I am completely innocent, and made me stay here for more than four months without proof or a single cause. Through this the spread of the gospel was greatly hindered and God's name was blasphemed far and wide. The Catholics were very happy and nurtured the hope that the work which had begun would now be destroyed. The Malabarian heathens and the Mohammedan Moors were angry about such procedures and were scared away from us, but since they recognized my innocence even better than I did they felt great pity for me, were astonished at my patience and waited eagerly to see how it would all end. Among the European Christians the common people were greatly dismayed and were not at all happy about such injustice, but they were not allowed to show it on the threat of punishment. Our European neighbours, namely the Dutch and the Englishmen, were also angry and said that it had never happened before that a preacher among the protesters had been imprisoned here in East India, and that this could never happen till they had first been condemned to it in Europe by the entire Church council. In the meantime, I remained calm in the face of my woes, praised and glorified God in my prison cell and, I must confess, that I have never before had such peaceful and pleasant days on earth and will hardly have them in future as I did in my prison cell. However, I would have liked to be able to work there on the Malabarian translation of the New Testament, which I had begun earlier. To this end I petitioned the commandant several times to allow me to do this work in prison, but even though as Christians they should have been happy about such holy work, they continued with their fuming and raging and did not listen to my pleas. They also did not allow those books of the Christian doctrine that I had translated into the Malabarian language to be unsealed and used for the benefit of the congregation by my colleague. Although they allowed me neither a Malabarian writer for the translation of the Holy Scriptures, nor ink, paper and quill, God ordained it in a wonderful manner that after a month I got white lead and paper so that I had the opportunity to edify my fellow-men in writing. Thus, through God's singular grace, I could write two books without the knowledge of my enemies, namely this book about the estate of the clergy pleasing to God and later another one about a Christianity pleasing to God. I know that many books containing similar matter have been written and edited in Europe so that my views about it are not required. I am also aware that it is not appropriate for my final purpose and my holy ministry here among the heathens to spend my time writing books in German. However, because they were written in my prison cell where, if I had not done this, I would have had to spend my time without edifying my fellow-men. I hope that no one will take it amiss if I send this book to my fatherland to have it printed. I am doing this for the benefit of the Christian Church and as a constant reminder of my woes to awaken many pious souls and to call on God unceasingly to bless me and the continuation of this holy work. Because this present book is about the estate of the clergy pleasing to God and is written for the edification of my teachers and that of other faithful teachers, I have made bold to dedicate it to all faithful witnesses of the truth in Denmark and Germany, but especially to you, my venerable Fathers in Christ Jesus and to you, my esteemed friends! I am certain that you will receive it graciously as a mark of the filial love that I bear for you. You are the ones through whom God imbued my soul with great mercy and compassion. Through your faithful instruction, good supervision and advice I could become

God's instrument. With your help I found the correct path to achieve true wisdom and bliss. Through you God found me worthy of working among the heathens. Your salutary advice and untiring care have contributed greatly to the work of the Lord among the heathens. Your unceasing prayers have done more for this than our own work. Remembering your holy example in all kinds of affliction and suffering has always encouraged us to be patient in our own distress. Our congregation praises your active love and helping hand and is sure that in future too it will have the pleasure of your goodwill and affection, and its numbers will increase. Therefore, I can say in all truth that everything good that has been done here among the heathens—and all that will still be done—can be ascribed not only to us, but also to you and to God's grace, since all this is a result of the salutary teachings we received from you and the good advice you gave us. Since this book is also a   fruit of your efforts and work on my behalf, it is my filial duty and obligation to dedicate it especially to you with the humble request that you look on it as a constant reminder of the Lord's work among the heathens and that you continue in your love, goodwill and affection towards me and towards our newly-planted congregation. In addition, I also hand over this testimony of the truth to all other faithful teachers and witnesses of the truth in Denmark and Germany with the assured conviction that although I know very few of them personally, I still bear a warm, sincere and brotherly love for all of them. I also wish from the depths of my soul that all of them with their combined efforts will help in the propagation of the Christian dogma among the heathens through constant prayers with their congregation, through all kinds of deeds and advice, but also through external aids and collection of generous donations from their congregations who should be happy that the light of the gospel has begun to shine among the heathens. As proof of their joy they should be able to contribute a little from their abundance to set up all kinds of good arrangements. Their love and serious efforts will help a lot in promoting our holy ministry among the heathens. Along with my other three colleagues I would be very happy and encouraged to further untiring efforts if I were to hear that Protestant universities and Church councils as well as all other faithful teachers and preachers in Europe appreciate this holy work and show it through deeds. Even though till now I have had to undergo a lot of misery for the sake of this holy work and can see that more distress awaits me, I am of good cheer, and the more I am persecuted by the kingdom of darkness, the greater will be the strength that God will give me. I also hope that my imprisonment will bring me honour from God and all faithful witnesses of the truth in Europe. For the rest, I herewith assure all pure Protestant theologians that in the Malabarian language of the heathens here I propagate only the pure dogma of Jesus Christ as it is written in the word of God and in our Libris Symbolicis (i.e. the Lutheran symbolic books) and as I propose to account for before the tribunal of Jesus Christ. Because, despite the fact that there is no one, neither here nor in Europe, who can examine what I teach among the heathens, both verbally and in writing, you should all know, as you can see from this book and from my other writings, that all my life I have sought to teach only what is based in God's word. At the same time, I do not consider myself to be without weaknesses and defects. Therefore, if something should be corrected here and there in this book, I give everyone the liberty to tell me about it, and I will gladly let myself be informed about reasonable matters. However, I request that the conditions of my distress while writing this book be taken into consideration so that one does not get angry, given my youth, about the corrections of the many instances of misuse that have crept into the estate of the clergy and one does not judge the book wrongly. Because, I can say in all truth that I am not talking about particular individuals and neither have I let myself be driven by carnal feelings. Rather, while contemplating the enormous damage that stems from the deterioration of the estate of the clergy, I have been compelled by my conscience to present the truth in such a way as I considered necessary at that time in the light of the Holy Spirit and without any fear. No honest theologian can take exception to the fact that I have shown an earnest zeal in this book as well as in my official duties in repudiating those enemies of God who till now have strongly opposed this praiseworthy work among the heathens, especially when one considers those circumstances that led me to be zealous and often filled me with great anxiety. Thus, I could not be silent without violating my conscience and seriously impeding my ministry, even if it should cost me my life. Therefore, before one can judge everything that has happened here till now between the commandant and us one should be properly informed about everything that has occurred from the beginning till now for the sake of this work. Otherwise one is likely to be hasty in judging my serious acts as immature zeal. God knows that in my entire life I have had no desire to fight, neither verbally nor in writing, and I would have gladly tolerated and put up with whatever they wanted me to do if they had only attacked me personally and left my ministry unhindered. But, because they have attacked the whole work, have tried to throttle it with force and destroy it against the all-merciful will of our God and our king, I would have perjured myself before God and my most gracious king if I had not drawn attention to it and had accepted everything in silence. However, even if I have had to suffer great disgrace and humiliation on this account, I will refrain from bringing charges against my enemies either with God or with my most gracious king. Rather, I will present matters only in the way they happened and leave it in all humility to their most gracious will to take whatever action they wish against these people. I have no other wish than to see the work of the Lord promoted among the heathens in whatever way it can happen. Now, my dearly beloved fathers, friends and patrons and all faithful witnesses of the truth, since I have poured out my heart to you and have shown the love, respect and filial faith I have for you, I hope that you will continue to find me worthy of your love, goodwill and kindness and will help me at all times with advice and deeds in my difficult official work in the assurance that the greater the opposition to this holy work the more God will lead it to greater glory. May the Lord let the light of his gospel shine brightly among the heathens here and may his mercy ensure that even there in Europe through your faithful work with the gospel the merciful kingdom of his Son spreads and the knowledge of salvation is brought to many thousand souls for the honour, praise and glory of his holy name and for our well-being here and in eternity. Amen!

This is the heartfelt wish

For my dearly beloved Fathers
and all faithful witnesses of the truth.
Bound with you in prayer and love
Bartholomäus Ziegenbalg,
Servant of the divine word among the heathens in the congregation of Jerusalem.
Written in East India
on the Coromandel Coast at Tranquebar 1709
August 14th.

I.N.I.

May God grant the beloved reader mercy and compassion for his temporal and eternal well-being!

I still remember that in the course of my Christianity as well as in my study of theology I was inspired and encouraged when I read or heard with proper reflection about the wonderful guidance that God always gave to his faithful servants and friends in the world. Therefore, I think it is useful if, instead of a preface, in praise of divine grace and for the encouragement of the Christian reader I talk about all the wonderful guidance I have received since my youth through God's wise direction.

I was born on Midsummer day in the year 1683 in Pulsnitz which lies in the Oberlausitz on the border to Meißen. My late parents were taken away from me early so that I hardly knew them. But I still remember how my mother on her death-bed called all of us children to her and said: Dear children, I have collected a great treasure for you. My oldest sister asked her: Dear mother, where have you kept this treasure? She replied: Search for it in the Bible, my dear children, you will find it there. Because I have bedewed each page with my tears. This moved us children deeply and we often talked about this with one another.

I was raised by my oldest sister and was made to go to school and to diligently read God's word. God then began to work powerfully on my soul so that I could never banish thoughts about heaven and hell. My heart endured severe punishments when I had done something wrong. When someone died, I always wondered where his soul might have gone to! What changes might it have undergone? After I had resolved to study this I often went to the fields and hills, fell to my knees and asked God to give me wisdom.

In the meanwhile, I went to school in Kamenz where I was exposed to many temptations of a worldly life, but the severe punishments of my conscience held me back from many sins. From this school I went to the high school in Görlitz where I received tutelage from Herr Magister Samuel Großer. My intention was to study theology, but I had not organised my studies properly and did not know how to organise these in order to achieve my final goal. Therefore, I spent a lot of time on useless things.

When I was sixteen years old a student came to me just as I was holding a Collegium musicum[1] and he said that music was indeed a magnificent art, but it could only be properly understood and used by someone who was in spiritual harmony with himself and with God. I liked what he said and asked him what he meant by spiritual harmony? He then told me how the spirit was in a state of confusion after the fall of man and how it had to be arranged quite differently if a proper harmony was to be established again. I felt a great love for this person, took him in and asked him to honour me with his friendship. He agreed to do this but stipulated that I should avoid the friendship of the world. I replied that I would gladly submit to his guidance and directions. Thereupon I opened my heart to him and asked him to advise me on how to be a proper Christian. He replied that

---

[1] A private gathering of music lovers.

all wisdom and all good gifts came from God. Now God, for his part, would be willing and ready to give his gifts to everyone, but he encountered a lot of opposition since many people did not want to submit to his holy order. Therefore, if I wanted to be a recipient of his gifts and his wisdom, I would, above all, have to strive to ensure that my soul was in a condition that was pleasing to the triune God and I could then be part of his holy community. Then, everything that I began in his name would go well. I approved of all this but asked how I could reach such a state. He then told me how God had brought him to it in a wonderful way and suggested three means to achieve this, namely, to pray with me daily, to discuss God's word and to lead me to the book of nature. I was very pleased with this and I began to pray with him daily, discussed God's word with him every day and then went with him to the fields where he showed me how one can take delight in observing God's creatures and use every creature as a lesson.

Having associated with him in this way for some time I learned that my earlier Christianity had been false and hypocritical. I, therefore, began to lead a completely different life, avoided all company and took sincere care of my soul. But, when the other students noticed this, they began to mock and jeer at me in all kinds of ways so that even my faithful friend was worried that their slander might hinder me in my good resolutions. He therefore asked me to go on a journey with him, on the one hand, to put some distance between the others and myself, but, on the other hand, to become more firmly grounded in the truth through God's word and the edifying contemplation of God's creatures. When we had finished our journey and returned to Görlitz I had to see and hear how not only my fellow students but also many others mocked and jeered at me. However, I was now more firmly grounded in the truth so that they could not achieve anything with their slander except to take me closer to God. My soul had tasted so much sweetness and joy in God that it could now not only deny the desires of this world, but also willingly tolerate its hate and contempt.

At this point the guidance of my faithful friend came to an end. However, I was not abandoned by God's hand which had taken hold of mine in mercy and had led me on the path of life. It continued then to guide me on the path of good. I led a quiet and withdrawn life, went about daily in deep reflection, prayed and allowed the contemplation of the divine word to be my constant pleasure and joy. It was then that I properly understood the words that my late mother had spoken to us children on her death-bed, namely that we should look for her collected treasure in the Bible. Therefore, I also exhorted my sisters through letters to obey the will of our mother and, along with me, search for the heavenly treasures in God's word.

But the greater the strength and mercy that I received from God, the stronger was the opposition of the world against me, especially since I now also began to punish its sinfulness and its hypocritical Christianity. However, after I had enjoyed God's mercy for some time and through it had won some victories over the devil, the world and my sinful flesh and blood, the most severe temptations began in earnest. It was as if God had abandoned me, for I could not feel his comforting presence in my soul. On the contrary, I saw in me and in all people only wretchedness, misery and sorrow. It was then that my eyes were really opened to the deep corruption of the children of men and I was highly astonished, on the one hand, about God's great forbearance in sparing this godless world instead of meting out just punishment. On the other hand, I was astonished about the ill-nature of men and that they could still be so proud, shameless and assured in the face of their misery. I could not speak with anyone of the deep inner distress of my heart and did not have anyone to whom I could reveal the condition of my heart since everyone believed it was only melancholy which had to be driven away by carnal pleasures. I was disgusted by everything in the world and could find peace and pleasure in nothing. My teachers saw me going around in great sorrow and in such physical weariness that they did not know what to do with me. Despite this, they loved me more than I deserved.

After I had suffered great distress of my heart for 9 months and, by wrestling and struggling, had been tested and purged by God, the delightful and comforting light of the holy gospel again began to shine in my soul and become a proper evangelical joy. However, I now had to struggle with myself since I did not know whether it would be advisable to continue the study of theology considering both the heavy responsibility and the very deep corruption in the estate of the clergy which I became aware of at that time. Nevertheless, I also overcame this challenge and thought that for this very reason it was even more necessary to study theology because there were such few faithful workers. When I thought about the great benefactions that God had granted my soul in this one year, I realised that I was now obliged to dedicate myself fully to serve him and to seek nothing more in this world than the glorification of his holy name. However, I also saw that this could only happen through service to my fellow-men that they may also be saved and brought into the community of the triune God. I realised that to achieve this I would have to become qualified to be of service to God and my fellow-men. Therefore, I began my studies in earnest. Now, everything seemed to be easy, since God had changed the disposition of my mind.

I organised my studies in such a way as to reach my final goal at the earliest. Besides this, I also began a correspondence with pious, wise and learned theologians, told them about the guidance I had received and asked them for their advice. Through their letters I became even more inspired, and this promoted my studies. I had divided my studies and my Christian devotions into particular hours. Along with the study of languages I devoted myself specially to reading and contemplating the divine word. The theological books I loved most were those that led me closest to the Holy Scriptures. Although I listened to the treatment of philosophical disciplines, my conscience found a lot of contradictions in them. I devoted myself to learning ethics and physics from the Holy Scriptures and, for the latter, the Comenii Physicae was also very useful. I found that all the things one could see were named in God's word together with their spiritual application, and I learnt here with great joy about the beautiful and delightful harmony between the kingdom of mercy and the kingdom of nature. All creatures reminded me of what I had read and contemplated in God's word. I spent two years in such devotions while tolerating all kinds of insults, ridicule and mockery from those worldly people. In the meanwhile, I also tried to make the most of my few talents and considered it a great joy if I had the opportunity to edify my fellow-men through words or letters. God did not fail to bless these good intentions.

From this city Görlitz the late Herr Dr. Spener and Herr Magister Joachim Lange called me again to Berlin and I finally followed their advice. I enjoyed faithful tutelage under the guidance of Herr Magister Lange so that I now began to gain proper solidity in my studies. I heard the principles of true wisdom so purely and clearly that I was greatly delighted. There was also no lack of edifying exercises in piety for us students since we held a Bible class amongst ourselves and, both publicly and privately, we were instructed in the practise of a true Christianity by our rector. At the same time, we also had the liberty of revealing our condition to him and telling him about all cases of doubt. I can say with certainty that besides the help of God I made progress in my studies on account of the good guidance of these teachers and the very gifted writings of the late Herr Dr. Spener.

After I had enjoyed their paternal love to my advantage for some time God saw fit to afflict me with a persistent illness so that I was forced, against my will, to travel to my Fatherland in order to let my sister take care of me. Despite this, however, their salutary letters and edifying writings continued to help me in my studies. Since I had to spend a whole year with my eldest sister and since my ailment was such that I could continue my studies to some extent, I repeated everything that I had learnt in schools and high-schools. I also tried in all kinds of ways to use my talents on my fellow-men, both verbally and in writing, especially since I always thought that my life-span would be very short and, therefore, I hurried even more towards my main purpose. And, even though I was often reminded, both verbally and in writing, to look after my health, I thought it was better to have lived a short and good life than a long and worthless one.

Wherever I was, the affliction followed me everywhere, but in a way that I could always bear it patiently. When my body had gained a little strength, I visited different universities, but I liked the one in Halle best. I organised my studies according to the advice of the professors there and noticed a blessed progress in all. But, just as had been the case when I was in school, dealing with God's word was my main work, and I let this be my joy and delight also at university. Therefore, I sought out like-minded fellow students who shared my final goal and with them I dealt every day with God's holy word at meal times. Besides this, we also held a Bible class twice weekly among ourselves in which everything was geared towards our edification. The professors were like faithful fathers to us and always showed us the shortest and the easiest way to gain true wisdom.

However, with every new day the deep corruption in the estate of the clergy became increasingly apparent to me and I was also struggling with great weakness of the body. Therefore, I was again in a state of confusion and for a long time had grave doubts about whether I should continue my study of theology or whether it would not be better to devote myself to life in the countryside so that I could live in peace and save my own soul instead of taking on the burden of the souls of others. I was almost in the same situation as Jonah who also wanted to be freed from a heavy burden, but finally had to obey God's command. Although I was not thrown into the sea like Jonah, I was made to feel the hand of God through hard punishments so that I finally had to yield to God's will.

Because of my indisposition, however, I was forced to leave the university at Halle for some time and go to Merseburg where I found a good opportunity to work with God's holy word with young and old alike. I hope that this work is still a rich blessing for many of them. But, since the work was becoming too much for me, I took a good friend from Halle, Christian von der Linde, as my assistant. His heart and mind were linked closely with mine and with his talents he proved to be very useful there.

From there I was called to Erfurt. My faithful friend accompanied me a large part of the way, and under open skies we made this covenant that both of us would seek nothing else in this world than the glorification of the divine name, the propagation of the divine kingdom, the spread of divine truth, the salvation of our fellow-men and the constant sanctification of our own souls wherever we were in the world, even if we were to encounter distress and suffering because of it.

I then reached Erfurt and found all kinds of opportunities there to edify my fellow-men, but because of my physical weakness I could not remain there longer than two months. I was, therefore, forced to return to my Fatherland where, similarly, I did not lack for opportunities to edify my fellow-men through God's word. However, even here, as everywhere else, I was loved by the pious but despised and falsely judged by worldly people. Yet, I hope that for many people the association with me and dealing with the divine word will still be bringing them rich blessings. I again went through all the genera of my studies and brought them into a definite order. After that I searched through all philosophical disciplines, but found only whims in them, with which earlier monks with a lot of free time on their hands had complicated and obscured what God's word and nature present in an easy and clear manner. However, I was astonished about the theological systems which contained more terms from heathen philosophy than phrases from the Holy Scriptures and had thus made a heathen philosophy of the prophetic and apostolic theology. Indeed, when I read God's word in its purity, delight and clarity and compared it to these theological systems I was very surprised at the foolishness of men who sought, to their own detriment and with great effort, to make an easy thing difficult. But I discovered a very good Modum Philosophandi (manner of philosophising) for myself in the medicina mentis (medicine of the mind) of my very esteemed teacher, which gave me a keenly-desired guidance for the contemplation of spiritual and natural truths.

When I had carried out my studies quietly in this manner for almost a year and my physical strength had improved, I decided to go to universities again. However, just as I was getting ready to leave, I unexpectedly got the sad news that my youngest sister had died. I, therefore, first had to go to her funeral with my eldest sister. On the way my eldest sister urged me to stay another year with her and study on my own since only the two of us were left and since I tended to be sick and ailing. Although I had some misgivings, I agreed on the condition that I would first travel for two or three months in order to get to know wise and learned men. Then, around winter, I would, God willing, return to her. I parted from her and travelled to Berlin. There I was encouraged by a preacher to temporarily take his place in the church and school in Werder, 5 miles from Berlin, since he had planned a journey and marriage. I accepted this opportunity with great delight, and for eight whole weeks I tried to apply all the hard work I was capable of in the church and the school.

In the meanwhile, Herr Dr. Lütkens wrote from Copenhagen to some preachers in Berlin that His Majesty, the King of Denmark, had salutary thoughts and had graciously resolved to send some missionaries to East India, West India and Africa in order to give the heathens an opportunity to convert from their damnable darkness to the true God. If any capable people were available, they should be sent as soon as possible to Copenhagen. Many were delighted with this news, and they diligently looked for students of theology who could go there. Among others, even my humble person was suggested, but they did not know where I had gone till, by chance, they received news from me, upon which they told me about the offer. I, however, saw it as a temptation sent by God, and although I did not outrightly reject it, since I wanted to submit to their good advice and wishes, I presented them with some considerations and thought that they would spare me from this.

Yet, when I came to Berlin again three weeks later and believed that capable people would have already been found for this holy work, I heard for the first time that they placed all their hopes in me. First, I presented my lack of qualifications and said I had decided to spend several years more at universities. Secondly, that I was too young for it and had scruples about taking on such a high and important job. Thirdly, I was always ailing and would hardly be able to endure such a difficult journey. Fourthly, my physical condition was such that I would not be able to arrive at a decision quickly. They were, however, able to remove all my doubts and to present the matter in such a way that I could no longer refuse with a good conscience.

Besides me they had chosen another pious student called Herr Heinrich Plütschau who in high school and at university had been my close friend. I joined him in prayer and we both tried to understand God's will and advice. When our dear former teachers, namely Herr Magister Lange as also Herr Lysius and Herr Kampe, along with all the other preachers there, made it clear to us that we should not refuse such a divine profession so that our conscience would not trouble us for the rest of our lives for this disobedience, we both finally decided in God's name to accept this profession. We then only requested that we may be allowed to travel to our Fatherland and bid farewell to our friends. But even this wish could not be granted since more letters had arrived from Copenhagen saying the matter was urgent. We, therefore, denied ourselves even this and took leave of our friends through letters.

When we had received everyone's blessings and had been entrusted through prayer to God's mercy, we left Berlin on October 8, 1705 and arrived in Copenhagen on October 15 where we got a friendly welcome from Herr Dr. Lütkens. Both of us had never lacked for troubles and challenges in Germany, and these followed us to Denmark, so that there too we were not without challenges. But we remained passive concerning everything and finally, on the orders of His Most Gracious Majesty, we were ordained by Herr Dr. Bornemann and told to go as missionaries to East India.

We then boarded our ship, Sophia Hedwig, on November 29, and the help and protection of the God of nature accompanied us. Even though we often faced difficult challenges, we were always richly comforted by God. The ship was a very useful university for us where many mysteries in the book of the Holy Scriptures and in the book of nature were revealed to us. In order to pass time in a more edifying manner I began a daily meditation about all the truths that I had heard in schools and universities or had read in God's word and in other books, while also examining myself as to how far I had come in the practise of these truths. When we were close to different dangers on the high seas, I could find no consolation either in logics or in metaphysics or in the other philosophical disciplines, but only in God's word. O! I then really began to thank God from the depths of my heart that he had given me the proper love for his word from my youth onwards and had always shown me such love that I had used most of my time in schools and universities contemplating his word.

After we had safely reached Cabo de Boa Esperanza and had sailed from there again, I began my meditation on the matter of true wisdom which I loved so much that I decided to write down such meditations and communicate them to my fellow-men. In this way I wrote most of the book called Allgemeine Schule der wahren Weisheit, which I later added to and sent to Denmark in 1707.

When we reached here safely on July 9, 1706, we started to learn the Portuguese and Malabarian languages. God blessed everything that we began in his name. However, the devil saw that this holy work would diminish his kingdom and so he opposed it with all his strength and sought to persecute us through his instruments, But, by now we had already faced all kinds of trials and were, therefore, more than willing to take on trouble. God allowed one soul after the other to be saved from their blindness and gave us the opportunity to work with his word on the European community here, both publicly and privately, so that we could not praise God's blessings enough.

However, we always encountered stiff opposition not only from the heathens but also from the European Christians. The commandant and the whole privy council became adversarial to the extent that they would not only not help us in anything, but they also tried to hinder this holy work in all kinds of ways. We had decided to build a small church at our own expense, but they strongly opposed this, so that we were finally forced to make their un-Christian behaviour known, both privately and publicly. But they were not moved, either by our entreaties or by our zeal. Therefore, we had to build a church against their will in the name of our God and our most gracious king. This plan was successful and led to great progress in our work. We began to preach twice every Sunday in the newly-built church and to catechise twice a week, myself in the Malabarian language and my dear colleague in the Portuguese language. Similarly, a Malabarian and a Portuguese school were set up. In this way our congregation grew every week and God also gave us more physical and spiritual strength so that even the most difficult work was a delight and joy.

Finally, heathens, Moors and Christians had to admit that this was a holy work. Yet, for all that, the ones in authority here did not want to recognise this, and continued in their hatred and envy, annoying even the heathens a little. It was impossible for us to silently overlook this un-Christian behaviour, and we had to say what our conscience demanded, especially because we saw that many hundreds of heathens were being hindered in their conversion because of this. But, the more we spoke the truth the more vehemently we were persecuted by them and their goal was to destroy us and our entire congregation, which they told us both verbally and in writing. They also forbade us to continue working either publicly or privately with the white congregation. We, however, continued our work of dealing with God's word happily and the white Christians desired even more to hear God's word, especially since we did everything for free and did not take a penny from anyone except what was contributed voluntarily for the upkeep of our church and schools. In the meanwhile, because we saw how fiercely they were acting against God and his holy work, we were finally forced to report all their actions to our most gracious king with the humble request for his merciful protection and help.

We had worked here for three-and-a-half years amongst a lot of opposition and our congregation now consisted of 100 people apart from those who were yet to be baptised. All European Christians were also very happy about this except for the authorities, who still opposed it, and all those who had to please them. In the name of the triune God I began to translate the New Testament into the Malabarian language and had reached the 23rd chapter of the gospel of Matthew. But, as soon as the Danish ship sailed away, the commandant looked for every opportunity to bring about what he had long threatened us with. We bore everything patiently, but we could not be silent, especially since this was not only an insult to God, but also to our most gracious king. We had sworn a three-fold oath in Copenhagen: firstly, that we would only propagate the pure word of God, secondly, that we would follow the instructions given to us to begin and continue this work with all seriousness and, thirdly, that we would observe the respect and well-being of our most gracious king everywhere. Therefore, our conscience demands that we talk about it and present the facts even at the cost of our lives.

Among other things, in the case of a poor widow in our congregation I had to write to the privy council, because a Catholic claimed that her late husband owed him 40 Reichstaler, but he could present no proof for this, neither in writing nor verbally. However, one was more well-disposed to the Catholic than to the widow in our Lutheran congregation and acted quite unjustly towards her, ordering her to pay half the amount. The widow with her old mother and two children complained very frequently to me and had quaint ideas about the Lutheran court of justice. However, I could not help her in any way and sent her away each time she came. But, since she tearfully lamented about her poverty and I also saw the injustice done to her, I advised her to plead humbly to the commandant to give her justice. Even though she went twice with her mother and two daughters, the commandant did not give her a hearing but directed her to us. She came to me tearfully and beseeched me to bring the matter to the high court because there was no other white person who could speak to her in her language. Thus, I was finally forced to take the matter to the high court with the request to appoint a guardian for such widows and to proceed in the matter without partiality or emotions, but only according to the laws of our most gracious king so that the impression is not created that only heathens and Catholics would get justice, but not those who had converted from heathenism and Catholicism to our Lutheran religion. This impression had angered many heathens already and had prevented their conversion. I wrote this letter while heaving many sighs to

God that it may have results and cause the authorities to reflect. However, Councillor Brunn handed over the letter immediately to the commandant who at once had my colleague summoned and had the audacity to say in his presence that he would take his revenge on me on the basis of his authority and show me in a few days the extent of his power, especially since he had been waiting long for such an opportunity. When my colleague told me this, we both fell onto our knees and prayed that either God change his mind or make me so cheerful that I could bear everything patiently.

On the same evening I was first summoned to the court and then to the Fort. Since the commandant had dealt with me very harshly twice before, almost resorting to something that he would have to eternally regret, I was advised not to see him unless there was a written summons which I could later use as proof if a mishap occurred, or unless he had me fetched by force so that those who came to fetch me could be witnesses. This was important since his only intention was to take his revenge on me and to cool his temper. I commended the matter to God and in our prayer-hour we were at the 16th chapter of the Acts dealing with the imprisonment of the holy apostle Paul. While explaining it I showed how this would be soon also done to us and, therefore, everyone should accustom themselves along with us to distress. In our church, however, I had to explain the 10th chapter of the evangelist Matthew, and I showed my congregation how the servants of God had always been persecuted and how this would now also happen in Tranquebar. After this I said a heartfelt prayer in front of the altar near the exit of the church and placed it in God's will whether he would, in future, let me set foot before such an altar. I was thus preparing to go to my death and told my colleague to do everything properly and to be of good cheer. After that I fell to my knees, prayed and wrote another letter to the commandant telling him how the matter was placed and that I would be quite willing and ready to come to him in the fort if he were to summon me in writing and question me in good faith in the presence of impartial persons so that this may, at a later date, be presented truthfully to my most gracious king. But, if for the sake of the truth, one wanted to needlessly put me on trial for slander and be prosecutor as well as judge, then I would appeal to my most gracious king, in whose name they would have to prosecute me, as on whom alone I depended and in whose work all this was happening to me. If, however, according to his threats, one wanted to use force on me, thus insulting God, our most gracious king and our Lutheran religion, also angering our European neighbours and hindering this holy work of God and of our dear king in the conversion of blind heathens, I would bear everything God inflicted on me patiently. However, anyone who wanted to do this should be warned that it would be his fault alone and not mine if the almighty God and my righteous king would also, hereafter, use force on him. God should nevertheless give the commandant wisdom and a mild spirit so that he is able to dispose of the matter in such a way that instead of the presumed bad things, only good things would happen. Upon receipt of this letter he sent someone to tell me that I should come to the Fort. I, in turn, sent a verbal message that he should summon me in writing and inform me of the reason for which I was being called.

Shortly thereafter he had the poor widow, about whose matter I had written, fetched by force by the guard without any cause. She was on her way to the Fort and only wanted to tell me first that she had been summoned there. I saw her anger and realised that only force was going to be used now, therefore I had even greater misgivings about going to the Fort. Soon after that they sent Secretary Attrup to me and again requested me to come to them. However, I remembered that only a few days ago they had sent him along with two Danish sacristans to us and had assured us through him that the child of a white father could be baptised in our church as had been requested. But, on the next day, after this had been promised by the secretary, the order was rescinded and the whole matter was set back. Therefore, I could not trust either their words or the secretary. I, therefore, repeated that they should send me a written summons which could be shown to His Royal Majesty. I could not depend on their words, especially because they could turn these around as they wanted. If they did not do this, I would appeal to my most gracious king before whom they could prosecute me if they had any weighty reason to do so. If they had me fetched by force, I would not reply to anything but leave the matter to a higher court.

The secretary, however, did not want to report what I had said and instead sent the servant of the commandant to him with the message that I did not want to come. Thereupon, they immediately sent Lieutenant Kröckeln with the guard. I asked if he had been told to take me by force. He said that I should go with him. No, I said, I would first like to know whether he had been told to take me by force. He replied that if I did not want to come, he would take me by force. I said, if it is to be done by force, I will come, but first wait a while so that I may pray to God for my enemies. I then went down on my knees with my dear colleague and became very ardent in my prayer so that many people on the street came running to listen to the prayer. But the commandant sent one messenger after the other to bring me to him. I did not allow myself to be disturbed in my prayer, and the lieutenant and the guard were very moved by it and spoke to me more mildly than before. But, when the commandant sent even more messengers, they finally dragged me away by force from my prayer with spears, swords and loaded rifles just as they would take a murderer prisoner. I went with them in my dressing-gown and was very cheerful.

When I had gone up to them in the Fort, the bridge was raised and the gates closed, which made me realise that their intentions were not good, therefore I did not reply to anything they asked me, because their conscience told them that everything I had written was true and needed no explanations except for them to vent their anger. If I had spoken and posed as a hypocrite, I would have made an enemy of God, but would still not have been able to get out of their clutches. But if I had presented the truth according to all the circumstances they would have changed into angry bears. Because, if they could not tolerate the written truth, they would hardly be able to tolerate it if I were to verbally present them with the truth in a harsher manner. Therefore, I kept my mouth tightly shut so that I could not speak and remembered the example of my Saviour who similarly let his silence be proof of his innocence before the ecclesiastic as well as the worldly court.

Finally, they had me taken to prison by Captain Jürgen Larsen and guarded closely by soldiers so that no one could talk to me. I went into prison happily and consecrated it with singing and prayer. In the meantime, all my things were sealed and two days later the soldiers were called to take an oath that they would have nothing to do with me and my colleague. My colleague was also forbidden to preach publicly as well as to continue the private prayer meeting. Some members of our congregation were also prohibited from attending our church. The whole town was dismayed at this tyranny and all Christians and heathens took great pity on us, although they were not allowed to show this on the pain of physical punishment. Our congregation became sorrowful and frightened, those who were yet to be baptised went away again. All heathens were scared away and saw this as a sign of a great judgment. Our Lutheran religion became the laughing-stock everywhere. The name of God and our Saviour was blasphemed, but God's punishment followed soon thereafter and the whole town found itself in the throes of a famine. Yet, the tyrannical hearts saw neither in themselves nor in others God's punishment but continued with their fury and rage so that our congregation was almost completely destroyed. However, there were still many hearts that lamented our situation and prayed fervently for us.

I found it easy to comply with the will of God and remained calm, sang the praises of God in my prison cell and saw how this moved the guards to great pity so that they almost always sang, prayed or read books in front of my cell. In the meanwhile, I sent a request to the commandant to allow me a Malabarian writer in my cell so that I could translate the New Testament into the Malabarian language, or at least grant that I could get ink, quill and paper in my prison cell. I also asked that my things be unsealed again so that my colleague could get those Malabarian books about baptism, the Holy Sacrament and the Christian doctrine that had been translated into the Malabarian language so that the Malabarian congregation could be built up again. But the commandant sent a reply that none of these three requests could be granted. Through Officer Kramer I again told him that I would be willing to accept this decision if he felt confident about answering to God and my most gracious king not only for robbing me of my freedom to carry out my public work, but also for not allowing me to use my talents in my prison cell to work on the conversion of the poor blind heathens.

When I saw that I was not able to achieve anything I stopped talking and devoted myself to the constant contemplation of the divine word. Because I saw that despite carrying out my ministry faithfully, I had encountered such severe persecution, I decided to meditate on the words of God about the clergy in order to console myself. I was very happy and encouraged by the fact that all men of God, both in the Old and the New Testament, had been persecuted for their faith and loyalty and had been imprisoned and killed as traitors, agitators and harmful people. I wished from the depths of my heart that I could communicate such meditations for the edification of my fellow-men and that my talents would not remain unused in prison. However, I was quite willing to be satisfied by my lot and regarded this as an opportunity for God to purify me and make me capable so that I could later serve him with even greater joy in his Christian Church. It was also an opportunity to gather divine strength for the future through prayer and heavenly contemplations.

After I had spent almost a month with great pleasure in the delightful company of God, I was woken up from my sleep one night by the guard who asked me whether I would like to have a white lead quill. I considered this to be a special sign from God and replied that it would be very useful, but that I did not have any paper to write on. Soon after, the person brought me a book of white paper and he told me that all the inhabitants of the town, both Christians and heathens, felt great pity for me, but had to leave the matter to the justice of God and of his anointed. I saw in this God's great goodness, and since my wish had been fulfilled, I began to write down the matter about the holy estate of the clergy and noticed every day that the triune God extended his friendly co-operation to me since I was abandoned by all men and could take refuge in none other than him. And this was the reason why I was compelled in my meditations to write only the pure truth as it was opened to me in God's word and through the enlightenment of the Holy Spirit, even though I could often foresee how one thing or the other would not be received very well by the world. However, I did not allow myself to be guided by the scruples of reason, but rather by the assisting grace of God knowing full well that God would never destroy my confidence in the truth of his words. Praying constantly, therefore, I continued with my work and was comforted by it amid my many tribulations so that I often wept tears of joy rather than of sorrow.

In the meanwhile, the conscience of my enemies awoke, and it appeared as if they regretted what they had done to me. The commandant invited my colleague as a guest and had wide-ranging talks with him, giving him proof of his esteem. When I heard of this, I wanted to help them set things right and so, on the New Year, I sent a message to the commandant that I would like to wish him for the New Year and whether he would like me to come to him, or whether I should pass on my greetings verbally through others. Upon this he sent me ink, quill and paper, excused himself saying he was not feeling very well and said that I should wish him for the New Year in writing. I did that without saying anything about my matter and only wishing him divine wisdom so that under his rule the work of our most gracious king may be promoted. He would see from all this that rather than hating him I only had love for him.

When he read my letter, he sent me the words of Solomon: Whoever seeks good finds favour, but evil comes to one who searches for it. Proverbs 11:27. I replied that in the end it would be proven who had sought good and who had searched for evil.

After three days he again sent someone to ask me whether I wanted anything else from him. I only needed to tell him, and he would do everything possible to help me. I thanked him humbly for this friendly offer and said that for the present I was living contentedly with my God and wished for nothing except his good health. However, if he would allow me to have a Malabarian writer so that I could work on the translation of the Holy Scriptures in my prison cell it would make me very happy. As far as my situation was concerned, I remained completely passive and placed everything in his hands. Thereupon he did not say anything to me again. His intention was to get me to request my freedom in order to show that not he, but I was responsible for my being in prison.

Since this was not feasible, he again invited my colleague as a guest and finally offered an amicable settlement if both sides were willing to consider it a mistake and a hasty action. The privy council agreed to this and would have liked to have seen me set free a long time ago. The second-in-command, Mr. Andreas Krahe, told my colleague that he was not responsible for my imprisonment and he would see to it that he, along with the other privy councillors, would wriggle out of the matter. However, he would now like to have an amicable settlement since he would then like to take me into his house as an angel of God. The amicable settlement would, however, have to be done in such a way that neither side said too much, and a handshake was arrived at quickly. Besides, the matter should not be reported to His Royal Majesty, because even if it were presented to him as a narrative of events and not as an accusation, it could still be considered accusatory. I should, therefore, ensure that peace and unity were restored. When my colleague then came to me and reported everything in detail, I did not wish to hinder the matter and said that I would comply with their wishes as far as possible, but it was not possible to leave the matter unreported to the king. This would be too dangerous for them and for me, especially since, according to my instructions I was bound by oath to give an annual account of everything that had happened in carrying out my ministry. If they, as his sworn subjects, were advising me not to report this, they and I would become perjurers. However, my colleague should only tell them that I would agree to whatever was possible for me. It then became certain that I would be free in two days, which the commandant himself told my colleague, and the whole town was happy. But, when my colleague goes again to the commandant and gives him my reply, he finds that the commandant has changed his mind and, thus, the matter was postponed again.

Eight days later, the commandant called my colleague again and was strongly opposed to everything, saying that he had no advice other than that I should explain my letters in writing and thus show what I had in mind. Thereupon, he would similarly explain himself in writing to me. In the meanwhile, however, he tried, through cunning, to bring my colleague over to his side and told him that he would be able to manage me alone. But he failed even in this, since my colleague's unity with me became more ardent the greater the persecution he encountered because of it. When, as they wished, he reported to me what I had to do, I took counsel from him and God and wrote the following letter to the commandant and the entire privy council:

Herr Commandant, Sir and the excellent Privy Council, highly esteemed Gentlemen.

It has been more than two months now since I was put into this, my prison cell, by you and I have not yet been summoned before the court for a proper trial despite the fact that in my last letter, even before my arrest, I had willingly offered to appear before the court if there was a complaint against me. According to the law of our most gracious king I had wished to hand the matter first to the lower court. On January 20, however, my dear colleague, Herr Heinrich Plütschau, was sent to me by you to make some suggestions for an amicable settlement, and I then sent you back the message that I would be passive in the whole matter and wanted to leave it to your disposition. After that, I do not know why the promised summons was again prevented. In the meanwhile, however, the esteemed commandant again called my colleague and demanded that I should give you a written explanation to which he would also reply in writing, upon which my colleague came to me again. In order not to cause any hindrance on my part, although I had grave doubts, I, nevertheless, at your request, asked for ink, paper and quill, and this was sent to me soon afterwards. I declare, above all, that I do not bear any hatred or enmity to your persons. Whatever I had to say and write to you in theological earnestness was required by the nature of my ministry and the obligation of my conscience towards God and my most gracious king. You will also find in yourselves proof that otherwise, in all matters of conversation, I have always been respectful, friendly and peaceable towards you. If, therefore, impartial persons, whether in the worldly or ecclesiastical court, were to properly consider what has transpired from the beginning till now in the praiseworthy and holy work of His Royal Majesty among the heathens here and, in this light, examine my two letters, one would not be able to lay the blame on me that I, as a servant of God, went too far against you in such matters. This holds particularly true when one considers what the prophets of the Old Testament did, whose example all honest teachers should follow in divine fervour even today if their ministry is guided by God not by men. Therefore, I also do not find it necessary to explain such letters at length, especially since in the words as also in the description of matters presented therein, they are written so clearly and lucidly that they can be understood without any explanations. However, if you still demand explanations, please send the letters to me and I will willingly give a long and detailed explanation with many examples. But before you ask me for this you should think about it carefully so that later you do not regret it when you read or hear my explanation. Just as I cannot believe that my letters are the cause of my imprisonment, I can imagine even less that my silence can be for you the reason for the same. As concerns the first, I had already explained clearly in my second letter that I would be willing to come to you if I was told in writing what one intended to do with me. I would not have demanded this if, two days earlier, one had not talked harshly to my colleague and told him how force was to be used against me. I also had many other reasons for it which I cannot cite now. As far as my silence is concerned, I can similarly give many reasons for it if I am asked. Therefore, I do not know why you have put me in prison and made me stay here for so long.

In the meanwhile, I will continue to conduct myself as passively as I have done till now, especially since the whole dispute concerns not only my person but, far more, the honour of my God and the respect of my most gracious king. If you wish to disgrace yourselves and prevent the work being done here among the heathens, who am I to stop you? And, if God wishes to throw me into hell for petitioning his honour, I will be satisfied and hope that my good conscience will create a delightful heaven for me even in hell. If even my most gracious king tells me to go to prison for petitioning his respect, my love for him and his most gracious wish will while away the time there. Therefore, I will take a chance with the most gracious will of my God and my king. However, if you wish to settle the matter here and either come to an amicable settlement or set up a judicial enquiry, I will gladly agree to it. If an amicable settlement is to be reached, I know of no other way of doing it than if both sides completely forget what has happened and only deliberate about the present and the future. As far as I am concerned, I am willing to forget my personal tribulations. But, as far as my most gracious king and my ministry are concerned, you will have to use your helping hand to compensate all that has been hindered in my ministry till now, so that one can report the matter to His Royal Majesty in such a way that you do not remain out of favour. The rest can be then discussed among ourselves verbally. I hope that afterwards, if it should come so far, the bond of love and peace between us will be stronger than what has separated us till now. If, however, you wish the matter to be decided by the court, I will willingly agree and hope that my love for your person remains unchanged, even if I would have to speak somewhat harshly against you in the matter at hand. But I do not know why I should sit here in prison for that, torn away from my holy ministry, especially since there is nothing to show that I have committed a crime heinous enough to deserve imprisonment.

However, if you find yourself affronted by my letters and, therefore, unnecessarily wish to bring action against me, a priest, for libel, it cannot justify keeping me away from my ministry and hindering the work of God and our most gracious king. This is particularly true since I would not run away but would remain steadfast till you had put into effect either here or in the Fatherland your imagined pretensions about me. If you have the wrong idea that I might run away, my dear colleague, Herr Heinrich Plütschau, is ready to stand surety for me, so that I can resume my work and he does not have to bear the burden alone.

He has often complained about this, especially since he is more in command of the Portuguese than of the Malabarian language and there are many in our congregation who do not understand any Portuguese. In addition, if I could be convinced that I deserve punishment, I believe that His Royal Majesty would have enough prisons in Denmark, so that without his order and without proof one may not put his most humble servant here into prison. If, despite this, you still want to let me stay in prison and spare no thought either for His Royal Majesty or for our newly-planted and hitherto growing congregation, I will bear this with great patience and pass my time in this cell most pleasurably with God. At the same time, I hereby declare for my omniscient God, for my most gracious king and for all Lutheran Christianity that I am pure and innocent of the blood of those heathens who will be lost because you have kept me away from my ministry.

Ah! Reflect well on what you are doing, especially since you are not fighting against me, but against God and your own king, who will never by vanquished by you. Think about what Lutheran Christianity in Europe would say if they were to hear that through you the propagation of the Christian Church here among the heathens has been hindered in this way! Consider also what the entire royal house in Denmark would think if it would hear the sad news that through its subjects such a holy work has been impeded in its expected progress, because in our vocation it is seriously forbidden on the pain of disgrace to stop or oppose such work. And, since I have reported to the royal house that I am working on a translation of the Bible and have, therefore, humbly requested a Malabarian printing press and have been assured that every year generous help for the promotion of this work will be sent by every ship, you must consider what will happen if you keep me away from my ministry any longer. Only God and my most gracious king who gave me this task can take it away from me. Indeed, consider what will happen here among Christians and heathens who are all very dismayed and have never heard of such things happening before. Since you are always concerned about the consequences of a matter, I request you to also consider what consequences will arise from this matter both here and in Europe, and even if you don't want to do it for my sake, please do it for your own sake! Especially since I am certain that one day you will thank me for this.

From all this you can see that I do not hate you, but that I am also not afraid of you and can write the truth in divine joy just as well in prison as I always did when I was free. I hope to remain cheerful as long as I do not seek to defend myself but only the truth. In the meanwhile, although you have denied me everything that I asked for, you have never been able to forbid me to pray for you, and you will never be able to forbid me this even in the future, and I will always remain

Bound in prayer and love to
the esteemed Commandant
and the noble Councillors.
Bartholomäus Ziegenbalg
Imprisoned servant of Jesus Christ
for the sake of the truth.
Written in Fort
Dansborg in my prison 1709, January 28.

I sent this letter to the commandant, who then called the entire council and the priests and held a consultation with them about the letter. But he has given me neither a verbal nor a written reply to it, rather he has shown himself hitherto to be even more hostile towards me and has also renounced all friendship towards my colleague.

In the meanwhile, I had satisfied my conscience and could continue the work I had begun in my prison with even greater joy. I wished for nothing except that the will of God prevail, who would not wish to destroy me, but would look to my temporal and eternal well-being. God gave me the required strength of body and mind and stood faithfully by my colleague so that with great courage and joy he could work among our congregation and maintain everything well. Thus, it happened that I finally completed this book about the estate of the clergy pleasing to God under the protection of the Almighty and without the knowledge of my enemies. I hope it will not remain without a blessing in the Christian Church as I have sealed all chapters with my prayers and tears. With this work I have no other purpose in mind than to promote God's honour and to awaken my dear fathers and fellow-brothers in the ecclesiastical estate as well as to comfort myself in my distress with the beautiful testimonies of the Holy Scriptures that have been cited.

When I had completed this book about the estate of the clergy pleasing to God and saw that I would still have to stay in my prison for a long time according to God's will, I began to write another tract about a Christianity pleasing to God. Just as I had almost completed this tract my colleague reported that my enemies would finally resort to extreme measures because they saw that we would never fall at their feet. Upon hearing this I asked God to tell me what was to be done. After praying, the thought occurred to me: See, if they are willing to go to the extremes of malice, you must make use of the extremes of love and do the opposite.

After some thought on how this could be done, I found it advisable to invite the commandant and his wife to my prison cell as guests. But I hardly believed that he would come, indeed I thought he would consider it a great affront because he was very angry with me and did not want to hear from me at all. But, at the given hour, God ruled over his heart and he sent the friendly message that he would come to me with his wife at the appointed hour. I still could not really believe this. No one in town could believe it either, but I had everything prepared and, finally, on March 17 he came to me with his wife. As soon as we saw each other we embraced and then we discussed our matter for a full seven hours at the table, on the condition that each of us would be at liberty to fearlessly say what he felt in confidence without either of us becoming bitter. I must confess that we had never told each other the truth in such detail as we did this time in prison. We finally concluded that things would have to change very soon. We then kissed one another and parted on good terms. I immediately wrote down the main points of our discussion in a letter and sent it to my colleague who replied that the whole town was astonished at this event and with this the heathens had been given an unmistakeable sign of our innocence, so that this would be a melodious bell that would resound over mountains and valleys through all of East India and Europe and would contribute greatly towards building our Jerusalem.

On March 23 the commandant had me fetched from prison and brought to him as his guest. After we had discussed sundry things he talked again about our matter and told me, because I had said that everything would have to be reported to His Royal Majesty, and they would then have to justify my arrest, he and the other councillors thought it advisable for me to give in writing that I be freed from my arrest and allowed to carry out my ministry again. I would also have to pledge an oath to remain here till the matter had been settled and that I would always appear where and when I was summoned. Then they would soon free me from prison.

I thought about this suggestion and immediately realised what they wanted. But I did not see how this could prejudice my cause, especially because they let it be known by this that they should have freed me immediately after my last letter to them in which I had asked for the same thing and had also named my colleague as my guarantor. I said, if the matter itself was not compromised I would gladly do this for the sake of my congregation. The commandant replied that the matter would remain as it is, and one could discuss it later and he did not see how this could harm him. Upon that I agreed and said that I would first send a draft of my letter to the commandant to make any changes he felt were necessary, so that he recognised that I was not only thinking about myself but also about him. I did this the following day and again made a fair draft of the copy on which the commandant had made some changes.

As soon as I had submitted this letter on March 26, I was summoned by an officer before the entire council. When I came up to them, they were all standing at the door. The commandant said: He shall now be free of his arrest. When I wanted to talk about various things, they changed the subject so that our matter was not discussed there. Thereupon I soon took leave of them and went to my house accompanied by Secretary Attrup. When my colleague had joyfully received me and all my things were unsealed, my children and the whole congregation gradually gathered together. Some fell at my feet and began to cry loudly, some greeted me with their hands and did not know how to express their joy. The Europeans did the same. There was great joy in the entire town.

God be praised for his salutary test and his wonderful guidance! May he now bless the work that I did with his help in my prison cell! May he awaken the Christian reader of this book with his spirit and encourage him to patiently bear all trials and suffering! May he give me and all honest theologians the spirit of joy that we may attest to his truth without the scruples of reason and despite all opposition in the assurance that he will protect and comfort us in his truth.

The Christian reader is also requested to join me in first thanking God fervently for the great benefactions he has always given me, but especially for showing me the opportunity to write this book in my prison cell and for helping me with the spirit of his wisdom and his strength. Secondly, the Christian reader should not take offence at my young age and, because of that, criticise and wrongly judge my sacred intention. Rather, he should join in my happiness that God allowed me to understand his mysteries through the stations of the cross and honoured me with these talents. Thirdly, he should not take exception to the simplicity of this book and to the fact that so many and such long passages from the Scriptures have been cited in it. Because, already two years ago, I declared in the preface to my Allgemeine Schule der wahren Weisheit that I would always use divine simplicity in all that I say both verbally and in writing, since it allows for far greater edification that high worldly scholarship. The reason why I have cited so many passages from the Scriptures is because I could find far more comfort in them than in my own words, and even at this young age I wish to edify my fellow-men with the word of God rather than with my own reason. From this it is almost immediately apparent that among the heathens I am only using the pure doctrine of the divine word. Fourthly, the kind reader will not take it amiss if here and there in this book he finds sharp reprimands for the malpractices that have been introduced in the Christian Church, especially since I have written all this out of compassionate love and not out of carnal feelings, which everyone can see from my situation of distress. If one reads my other book on a Christianity pleasing to God, in which I have refrained from all severe expressions and have mostly dealt with doctrinal matters, one will know that I like to use a gentle style. In order that a Christian reader profit from this book he should, fifthly, bring to its reading a heart that is devoted only to the truth and seeks only to find it and use it, always calling on God to unlock whatever scruples he may have in his heart. In the sixth instance he should, with God's grace, make every effort to avoid all those things in his work which he has understood from this book as being necessary to avoid. On the other hand, he should seek to do that which is useful and salutary for its promotion. In the seventh instance, if he gets any help from this book, he should think of my troubles and, with all devout theologians and pious Christians, should call on the merciful God to remove all hindrances in the propagation of the Christian Church and let the light of the gospel shine on the blind heathens for their conversion. Here among the heathens, I, for my part, will always think of all the faithful workers in Europe and will remain

United with the Christian reader
in prayer and love,
Bartholomäus Ziegenbalg

Written
in East India on the Coromandel coast
at Tranquebar
In the year 1709, August 17.

Prayer

O! you invisible and hidden God, you who leads his own in the world wondrously, but splendidly and wisely. I, your unworthy servant, have just cause to praise and glorify your name when I think of the kindness, mercy, love, loyalty and compassion that you have shown me in body and soul from my youth till the present hour. Because see! You followed me with your grace in my very difficult youth and did not stop working on my soul till you instilled in me obedience to your heavenly wisdom. Since then you have always firmly stood by me during my studies, you have enlightened me, taught me, filled me with divine light to understand your holy word, have given me many talents and, at the same time, have always proffered grace to practise a Christianity pleasing to you. Finally, you honoured me to carry out such a great and important ministry for propagating your salutary gospel to these heathens, for which you have hitherto given me boundless strength and grace. Therefore, I give praise, honour, respect and thanks for all such benefactions. I particularly extol your kindness at all times and that you tested and purified me through the many afflictions, sufferings, miseries, challenges and stiff persecution, drew me away from the world with all its vanities and directed my heart to the heavenly, eternal, spiritual and the future. You did not abandon me in my trials and tribulations and always comforted my heart, gladdened it, encouraged it in the joyful acknowledgement of the truth and protected it against all the might and power of my spiritual and temporal enemies. You showed me an opportunity in my prison cell to render a written account of your truth since I could not have done it verbally.

Because of all this I am now bound to always increase my knowledge of you, to love, respect and fear you, to serve you, to conduct myself according to your commandments and to walk down your paths, to always invoke you, to glorify your name, to use the talents received from you in all faithfulness and to strive with all earnestness in your strength that through me, unworthy servant, your name may be glorified, your kingdom extended, your truth propagated and the salvation of my fellow-men among Christians and heathens be promoted. For this purpose, I offer myself completely to you with body and soul and desire nothing more in the world than to be worthy of your friendship and company through which I will always hope to receive strength, grace, wisdom, kindness, love and comfort. I wish you to always show me opportunities to use my talents so that I may be able to complete the course of my life with joy. And, despite the fact that hitherto the world has not wanted to accept my testimony of the truth, instead has hated, envied, been hostile and has persecuted me, and finally locked me up in prison thinking it would stop me from talking and take away my good cheer, I do not pay heed to all this and do not allow myself to be hindered or disturbed in my intentions. Because you and your heavenly multitude are with me and are more well-disposed towards me the more you see me abandoned by men.

Now that you have armed me with the strength of your invisible eternity and have honoured me with the marks of your Son, Jesus Christ, have also hitherto given me richly of your favour and grace along with the assurance that you will never abandon or neglect me as long as I remain obedient to you, it is only fair that for your sake I deny everything in the world that will keep me away from your blessed company. I will also fervently strive to do everything that your word demands of me. Therefore, as long as there is still one warm drop of blood in my body, let me joyfully and without fear of men give evidence of your divine truth both verbally and in writing. Let me not care about the angry raging of the kingdom of darkness, not be afraid of any danger however great it may be, in the certainty that just as I try to defend your truth you, on the other hand, will defend me against all enemies.

Lord! Rescue your honour and never let me, your servant, be thwarted! Bless all the work that I, in the short span of my life in this world, have done with your word! But, especially bless what has been richly spread by me here among the heathens and lead your work among them to greater glory, the more it is suppressed and hindered by the devil and by the malice of men! Also bless this my work which I have written with many tears under your holy guidance and with the strength you gave me for the good of the Christian Church! Let all readers of this book be strongly moved, enlightened and comforted in their hearts by your truths and be encouraged to serve you in a fitting manner! Continue to show me all kinds of opportunities in the world that I may properly use the time still granted to me to lead many souls to you so that I may, in times to come, go gladly from this world into your invisible eternity to live there and praise you with all the holy angels and the chosen souls forever and eternally. Amen!

Amen!

TABLE OF CONTENTS OF ZIEGENBALG'S UNABRIDGED TEXT

The First Part of The Estate of The Clergy Pleasing to God: Dealing with its creator, its necessity, its excellence and importance, also with its order, difference and very acute deterioration.

The Second Part of The Estate of The Clergy Pleasing to God:
With instructions on how one can achieve a proper proficiency in it

> The first chapter: How one should apply oneself to piety from one's youth and organize one's studies befittingly

> The second chapter: How one should strive after true wisdom in the study of theology

> The third chapter: How in the study of theology one should always act on, read and reflect on God's word

> The fourth chapter: Why it is highly necessary in the study of theology to be taught by God

> The fifth chapter: How it is necessary in the study of theology to apply oneself to a lived understanding and real experience of all things that one must teach others later

> The sixth chapter: How a person should be tested and tried in the study of theology through all kinds of suffering and temptations

The Third Part of The Estate of The Clergy Pleasing to God:
Showing the principal characteristics of a teacher, how he should be, both inwardly and outwardly

> The first chapter: A teacher should be free of all wilful sins

> The second chapter: A teacher should be pious, god-fearing, godly and just

> The third chapter: In his work and his life a teacher should be humble

> The fourth chapter: In his life a teacher should be earnest

> The fifth chapter: A teacher should be irreproachable both in his teachings as well as in life

The sixth chapter: A teacher should be an example to his herd

The seventh chapter: A teacher should have a good conscience

The Fourth Part of The Estate of The Clergy Pleasing to God: Containing the most necessary requisites that should be found in teachers and preachers

> The first chapter: How a proper profession is necessary for a teacher
>
> The second chapter: How for every honest teacher the Holy Spirit is necessary
>
> The third chapter: How for every teacher a proper goal is required for his ministry
>
> The fourth chapter: How for a teacher and preacher a sincere love for God and his listeners is necessary
>
> The fifth chapter: How for a teacher proper loyalty to his ministry is required
>
> The sixth chapter: How for a teacher constant prayer is necessary in his ministry
>
> The seventh chapter: How for a teacher great joy is necessary in his ministry
>
> The eighth chapter: How for a teacher divine zeal is required in his ministry
>
> The ninth chapter: How for a teacher a good spiritual sense is required for dealing with the souls entrusted to him
>
> The tenth chapter: How for a teacher a proper management of his own household is required

The Fifth Part of The Estate of the Clergy Pleasing to God: Presenting the official duties or manifold functions of a teacher

The first chapter: About the first official duty of a preacher which consists in explaining the divine word, during which a teacher should be alone

The second chapter: About the second official duty of a teacher which consists in preaching

The third chapter: About the third official duty of a preacher which consists in teaching

The fourth chapter: About the fourth official duty of a preacher which consists in admonishing and warning

The fifth chapter: About the fifth official duty of a teacher which consists in punishing

The sixth chapter: About the sixth official duty of a teacher which consists in refuting erroneous ideas and defending the truth

The seventh chapter: About the seventh official duty of a teacher which consists in comforting

The eighth chapter: About the eighth official duty of a teacher which consists in his efforts to achieve an honest Christianity in his ministry

The ninth chapter: About the ninth official duty of a teacher which requires him to always point to Jesus

The tenth chapter: About the tenth official duty of a teacher which requires him to deal carefully with sacred property

The eleventh chapter: About the eleventh official duty of a teacher which requires him to make good arrangements in his ministry and to hold regular meetings with his fellow-brothers

The twelfth chapter: About the twelfth official duty of a teacher which requires him to take care of the poor

The Sixth Part of The Estate of The Clergy Pleasing to God: Showing what a teacher must avoid in his ministry

The Seventh Part of The Estate of The Clergy Pleasing to God: In which it is shown what fate faithful teachers and preachers tend to encounter in their ministry

The third chapter: Faithful teachers and preachers are always blamed and badly judged

The fourth chapter: Faithful teachers and preachers are often considered as people who confuse and lead others astray

The fifth chapter: Faithful teachers and preachers are generally despised, hated and envied by the world

The sixth chapter: Faithful teachers and preachers must be the laughing-stock of the world, they are ridiculed and slandered and troubled in many ways

The seventh chapter: Faithful teachers and preachers are very tormented people

The eighth chapter: Deliberations are conducted against faithful teachers and preachers and action is often brought against them

The ninth chapter: Faithful teachers and preachers are often beaten, imprisoned and even killed

The Eighth Part of The Estate of The Clergy Pleasing to God: Presenting that glorious comfort that faithful teachers and preachers can get in their ministry

The first chapter: God is closely linked with faithful teachers in their ministry and works through them

The second chapter: God cheers up faithful teachers and preachers with his comfort

The third chapter: God hears the sighs of faithful teachers and preachers, does a lot for them and reveals a lot of his hidden things to them

The fourth chapter: God takes care of, protects and saves faithful teachers and preachers from all danger

The fifth chapter: God gives rich blessings for the work of faithful teachers and preachers in their ministry

The sixth chapter: God rewards the work of faithful teachers and preachers in this world and in eternity

The Ninth Part of The Estate of The Clergy Pleasing to God: About the different names for teachers, about what should be observed while selecting them, what one owes them and what one should think of godless teachers as well as of false prophets

The first chapter: About the different names for teachers and preachers

The second chapter: What should be considered while selecting teachers and preachers

The third chapter: What one owes to faithful and honest teachers and preachers

The fourth chapter: How a godless or unconverted teacher cannot teach anything suitable

The fifth chapter: About false prophets

The First Part of The Estate of The Clergy Pleasing to God (Abridged)

Dealing with its Creator, its Necessity, its Excellence and Importance, also with its Order, Difference and very Acute Deterioration.

The First Chapter

About the Creator of the Holy Estate of the Clergy

§ 1. God had created man in such a way that he could recognise, love, respect and fear his creator as the well-spring of all bliss without the need for any teacher, and he had also created for him such spiritual strength that He could live, reign and rule in him. Therefore, it was not necessary for man to get outside instruction from this or that person since God himself was his teacher, enlightener, guide and leader, and thus he could understand all natural and spiritual things without any falsity and could use them for their proper purpose.

§ 2. Thus, we read in Genesis 2:16,17 that God the Lord spoke directly to Adam without any intermediaries and taught him, saying: You are free to eat from any tree in the garden; but you must not eat from the tree of the knowledge of good and evil, for when you eat from it you will certainly die. As long as Adam and Eve complied with this divine command and remained obedient to the holy guidance of their creator, they had no need for instruction from any creature apart from their creator who was intimately united with them.

§ 3. But after Eve listened to the serpent and through her disobedience parted, along with her husband, from God their creator, they not only lost the blissful companionship of their God and with it all wisdom, understanding and holiness, but they also fell into the greatest blindness, falsity, foolishness and sin, so that nothing was left in them except complete confusion of reason and a perversity of will. In this way, this misery was also passed on to all their descendants.

§ 4. God took pity on them and again spoke directly to them giving them the prophecy of his son who would squash the head of the serpent, and this God showed the means and ways through which fallen man could again be united with him, be taught by him and be blessed in him in this life and in eternity. Genesis 3:9. But he did not find proper obedience any longer in man. Therefore, although he loved Cain, he scolded him, saying: Why are you angry? Why is your face downcast? If you do what is right, will you not be accepted? But if you do not do what is right, sin is crouching at your door; it desires to have you, but you must rule over it. Genesis 4:6,7. But Cain remained angry and opposed the command and the salutary teaching of his creator.

§ 5. Despite the fact that God never stopped working on men so that they could be brought into a state where they would again allow themselves to be advised, instructed, enlightened, hallowed and guided in all truths by him, we find very few examples of those who were obedient, therefore he lamented: My Spirit will not contend with humans forever, for they are mortal; their days will be a hundred and twenty years. Genesis 6:3.

§ 6. When God, therefore, had punished the ancient world for its disobedience with the flood, he established a covenant with the pious Noah, whom he chose to be a preacher of righteousness before and after the flood. 2 Peter 2:5. Thus he began to act on men through men in order that at least some may be saved or so that all men would have the chance to convert from their sins and hereafter be without apology.

§ 7. After the pious Noah God chose the devout Abraham Genesis 12:1 and used him as his servant for the instruction of the lost children of men. Abraham faithfully obeyed God's command and began to preach about the name of the Lord, the everlasting God. Genesis 21:33,34. Thereafter God had such teaching continued by Isaac, Jacob and Joseph who preached the will of God to attain bliss. Not only did they do this in their own houses and families, but they also preached to all the inhabitants of their country.

§ 8. Finally, God appeared unto Moses in a fiery bush and, with great solemnity, appointed him as his servant and minister for the children of Israel, telling him: I am the God of your father, the God of Abraham, the God of Isaac and the God of Jacob. I have indeed seen the misery of my people in Egypt. I have heard them crying out because of their slave drivers, and I am concerned about their suffering. I am sending you to Pharaoh to bring my people the Israelites out of Egypt. Exodus 3:6,7. This mission was not only important to save their lives but also for the spiritual rescue of their souls.

§ 13. Therefore, the triune God alone is the author and creator of the holy ministry and, one after the other, has always had priests, teachers and prophets appointed properly through men. However, if the properly appointed teachers and prophets did not live in accordance with his will and did not want to present the truth to children of men in a befitting manner, he often inspired some teachers and prophets in an exceptional manner, as he himself says 1 Samuel 2:35. I will raise up for myself a faithful priest, who will do according to what is in my heart and mind. I will firmly establish his priestly house, and they will minister before my anointed one always.

§ 23. And to this end finally the son of God arrived in the world, so that he not only delivered us through his holy suffering and death, but also through his divine teachings showed us the way for attaining salvation. Therefore, he not only carried out this holy ministry himself with an untiring zeal and earnestness, but he also appointed his disciples to this ministry and sent them first to the cities of Israel while still associated with them. Matthew 10:1. Later, however, when he wanted to go from them to heaven, he gave them a general command and spoke: All authority in heaven and on earth has been given to me. Therefore go and make disciples of all nations, baptizing them in the name of the Father and of the Son and of the Holy Spirit, and teaching them to obey everything I have commanded you. And surely I am with you always, to the very end of the age. Matthew 28:18-20.

§ 24. Through many words and parables our faithful Saviour bore witness to this in his days as man that it was his heavenly father who had sent the real prophets and true teachers in the Old Testament Matthew 22:1, and even in the New Testament he promised to send many such teachers and faithful messengers when in Matthew 23:34 he says: Therefore I am sending you prophets and sages and teachers. Some of them you will kill and crucify; others you will flog in your synagogues and pursue from town to town. And this is really what happened afterwards.

§ 25. The holy Paul also received his apostleship from this Jesus when the latter appeared to him on his way to Damascus and later said to Ananias: Go! This man is my chosen instrument to proclaim my name to the Gentiles and their kings and to the people of Israel. Acts 9:15. Therefore, he writes about Jesus in Romans 1:5: Through him we received grace and apostleship to call all the Gentiles to the obedience that comes from faith for his name's sake. And Ephesians 1:9,10 he says: he made known to us the mystery of his will according to his good pleasure, which he purposed in Christ, to be put into effect when the times reach their fulfillment—to bring unity to all things in heaven and on earth under Christ.

§ 26. About this the holy apostle Paul further writes: 2 Corinthians 3:5,6. Not that we are competent in ourselves to claim anything for ourselves, but our competence comes from God. He has made us competent as ministers of a new covenant—not of the letter but of the spirit. And in the following Chapter 5:18-20 he speaks: All this is from God, who reconciled us to himself through Christ and gave us the ministry of reconciliation: that God was reconciling the world to himself in Christ, not counting people's sins against them. And he has committed to us the message of reconciliation. We are therefore Christ's ambassadors, as though God were making his appeal through us. We implore you on Christ's behalf: Be reconciled to God.

§ 27. It can be seen in the Acts, Chapter 13:2 that not only God the Father and our Saviour Jesus Christ but also the Holy Spirit was busy in this work. It says: While they were worshiping the Lord and fasting, the Holy Spirit said, "Set apart for me Barnabas and Saul for the work to which I have called them." Therefore, Paul later told the elders in Ephesus, Acts 20:28: Keep watch over yourselves and all the flock of which the Holy Spirit has made you overseers. Be shepherds of the church of God, which he bought with his own blood.

§ 28. Thus, it is the triune God who introduced this holy ministry in the world for the salvation of men. He not only sent faithful teachers at all times, but he also equipped them with the proper talents and gave his blessing and promise of thriving for their work, so that this holy order of God will be maintained till the end of time and that erring children of men will always have the opportunity to convert from the alliance with the Satan and with sin to the living God.

The Second Chapter

About the great necessity of the holy estate of the clergy

§ 1. The ruin into which man has landed after the deplorable fall from grace is so great and deep that not only is he completely incapable of rescuing himself from it, but he is also not able to properly understand this ruin on his own, nor develop the will to allow himself to be helped out of it. Therefore, if man were to live without instruction, without exhortation and without punishment, he would not have any concern for his soul, nor would he spare a thought for the coming eternity but would live in the day like an unreasonable brute, so that neither God's commandment nor the natural justice among the children of men on earth would be observed.

§ 2. If man should properly understand his misery and deep ruin and develop an earnest will to be freed from it; if he should learn to understand the nature and method of his salvation and the means through which he can once again attain the lost image, then it is necessary that he receives thorough instruction in all this from such persons who are experienced in the ways of the Lord and who have real knowledge of God's holy advice to the human race and who God himself has made capable of teaching the salutary word of truth.

§ 3. It is true that God does not need any mediators on his side to convert sinning children of men and he could deal with them himself and reveal his will to each of them. However, since fallen men cannot look at God's shining countenance because of their sinful nature and instead tremble and are frightened by the memory of him, it shows God's incredible benevolence to mankind that the majestic and invisible God deals with the timid children of men through men, and in such a way that men with their limited understanding can yet understand his divine advice and will in the easiest and clearest manner.

§ 4. Therefore, when God appeared to Moses on Mount Sinai and the people of Israel saw how the laws were given amid thunder and lightning making the whole mountain go up in smoke they fled, and from afar said to Moses: Speak to us yourself and we will listen. But do not have God speak to us or we will die. Exodus 20:18,19. Similarly, even all holy men were horror-struck and fell to the ground in shock when they heard a divine voice or even when they only saw the face of an angel. Therefore, it is necessary for men that God reveals his divine will through men.

§ 5. Saul too was horror-struck and trembled when the Lord Jesus appeared to him in a bright light. He fell to the ground and, trembling and apprehensive he said: Lord, what will you have me do? Because, however, the Lord knew that he would not be able to bear his brilliance if he spoke to him much longer, he said: Now get up and go into the city, and you will be told what you must do. Acts 9,6. What kind of a mediator did God use for his conversion? This is shown in the verses that follow when it says Acts 9:10-19: In Damascus there was a disciple named

Ananias. The Lord called to him in a vision, "Ananias!" "Yes, Lord," he answered. The Lord told him, "Go to the house of Judas on Straight Street and ask for a man from Tarsus named Saul, for he is praying. Ananias did make an objection, but he obeyed God's command, went there to the house, put his hands on him and spoke: Brother Saul, the Lord - Jesus, who appeared to you on the road as you were coming here—has sent me so that you may see again and be filled with the Holy Spirit." Immediately, something like scales fell from Saul's eyes, and he could see again. He got up and was baptized, and after taking some food, he regained his strength.

§ 6. We have a similar example of the Ethiopian eunuch who, on a journey, was reading the Prophet Isaiah and was, therefore, quite concerned about the salvation of his soul, but he could not understand the words of the prophet and needed some guidance. Therefore, the spirit of God spoke to Philip: Go to that chariot and stay near it." Then Philip ran up to the chariot and heard the man reading Isaiah the Prophet. "Do you understand what you are reading?" Philip asked. "How can I," he said, "unless someone explains it to me?" So, he invited Philip to come up and sit with him. And, since he had Chapter 53 of this Prophet open before him Philip began with this same scripture and preached the gospel of Jesus Christ to him. And, as they went on their way they came to some water and the eunuch said: Look, here is water. What can stand in the way of my being baptized? But Philip spoke: If you believe with all your heart, you may. He answered and spoke: I believe that Jesus Christ is the Son of God. And he gave orders to stop the chariot. Then both Philip and the eunuch went down into the water and Philip baptized him. Acts 8:36-38. Thus, Philip was the mediator through whom the eunuch became a believer.

§ 7. This kind of conversion we also find with the devout Cornelius who always prayed to God. Once he saw an angel of God coming to him, who said: "Cornelius!" Cornelius stared at him in fear. "What is it, Lord?" he asked. The angel answered, "Your prayers and gifts to the poor have come up as a memorial offering before God. Now send men to Joppa to bring back a man named Simon who is called Peter. He is staying with Simon the tanner, whose house is by the sea." He will tell you what you ought to do. Acts 10:3-6. Thus, the angel referred him to the instruction of a man and did not want to reveal God's will himself, showing thus how God not only honoured the ministry that he had created of the preacher, but also how important it was for men to be led and guided to God by men. Just as Cornelius obeyed God's command and sent for Peter so that he could finally be baptized by him along with all his near friends.

§ 8. Thus, he who scorned such a holy ministry and is of the opinion that he does not need the guidance of men for his conversion: such a person would find himself making dangerous mistakes and would be so opposed to God's will that he would later suffer from the lack of an opportunity that he had scorned, but one that he positively needed for his conversion. Because, even if we must firmly believe that God alone through his infinite power and mercy must convert the sinner, it is not easy to find an example in the world where a person was truly converted to God without any guidance from man. And, although he might not have been brought to the path of conversion by oral instructions from men, he would have to admit that either the word of God written by men or other edifying books initiated his conversion.

§ 9. The holy apostle Paul who had many extraordinary things to celebrate in his conversion writes in his epistle to the Romans that faith, and therefore the conversion of men, comes from the sermon or the preaching of the divine word. In Romans 10:14,15.17 he says: How, then, can they call on the one they have not believed in? And how can they believe in the one of whom they have not heard? And how can they hear without someone preaching to them? And how can anyone preach unless they are sent? As it is written: "How beautiful are the feet of those who bring good news!" Consequently, faith comes from hearing the message, and the message is heard through the word about Christ. With this the apostle clearly proves the necessity of the holy ministry.

§ 10. It is certain that if the estate of the clergy were to be abolished in the world, neither the ruling estate nor the civil estate would be able to exist for very long and one would see everything dissolving into disorder. One can see this to some extent in a city or a country where there are godless and unconverted teachers. In such places there are all sorts of vices and sins, so that one can find their Christianity only in the Bible and in other theological books, but their life is ten times worse than the conduct of the heathens. Therefore, David also asks in Psalm 12:7,8. You, LORD, will keep the needy safe and will protect us forever from the wicked, who freely strut about when what is vile is honored by humans.

§ 11. Just as a city or country is wretched when it does not have any or only impious teachers who are carnal-minded, that city or country is blessed which has pious, wise and faithful teachers who not only care for their own soul but are also deeply concerned about the eternal welfare of those entrusted to them. Although not all godless conduct will have been rooted out in such a place, one will find many who wrestle and struggle for the everlasting kingdom of invisible eternity, and one will see how the right fire of love has been lit among them, which gives rise to a movement to grow and increase in goodness.

§ 17. We see from the evidence cited here from the Holy Scriptures that the holy ministry is not only required for the conversion of sinners in order to shake them up a little with a sublime voice of penance, and to wake them up from their sleep, but that the same is also necessary for those souls that have converted, so that the work of conversion, of sanctification and renewal for the preparation of the divine image may be constantly continued. Because, when they once again have sin living in them and are tempted in various ways by the devil, the world and by their flesh and blood, they also need to be instructed further every day by the faithful ministers of God, to be comforted in their troubles, to be urged on in their laziness, to be punished in their disinclination and to be exhorted in their job of Christianity.

§ 18. Thus, the holy ministry is a necessary ministry for all kings, princes, regents and higher authorities. Also, for all teachers and preachers themselves so that they may be inspired and encouraged by others. Indeed, the ministry is necessary for all fathers, mothers, children and farm-hands, for the learned and the ignorant, for high and low, rich and poor, young and old, converted and non-converted, for Christians, Jews, Turks and heathens. One who understands this properly will honour such an estate and make the effort to be led to God through his ministers so that he may, both here as well as in eternity, achieve the bliss of the children of God.

The Third Chapter

About the Excellence of
the Holy Estate of the Clergy

§ 1. The ruling estate in the world is an excellent and very illustrious estate that has great worldly dignity, honour and grandeur. The civil estate too is a very laudable estate blessed by God. However, the estate of the clergy surpasses all of them in spiritual dignity, honour and excellence, and is thus not only the most necessary one in the world, but also the most blessed and magnificent estate, even though its excellence remains unrecognized by most people.

§ 2. The excellence of such a holy estate of the clergy can be seen from its creator, who is the triune God and who instituted it with great solemnity. He also initially raised it in its temporal and material dignity above the ruling estate and above all kingdoms and principalities, so that the people of Israel were meant to be ruled by the priestly class. As God himself says: you will be for me a kingdom of priests and a holy nation. Exodus 19:6. God always appointed capable persons to this priesthood and holy ministry, he joined with them and through them he glorified his name in the world by revealing his divine will through many signs and miracles, so that almost all the miracles that are written about in the Old and New Testament were only made possible by this holy ministry.

§ 6. In the New Testament, however, faithful teachers and preachers have far greater merit over the Levites of the Old Testament, especially since the ministry that gives of the spirit and preaches justice has far greater clarity than the ministry of the Old Testament which kills through the letters and preaches damnation. 2 Corinthians 3:7,8. In the New Testament a far greater sanctity has also been entrusted to them. Matthew 7:6. They do not deal any more with figures and shadows but with the essence itself. Hebrews 10:1. They have been given a firm prophetic word to preach. 2 Peter 1:19. They must preach such a sweet and wonderful gospel sent from heaven by the Holy Spirit, which even the angels desired to look into. 1 Peter 1:12.

§ 7. Besides this, all righteous ministers of Jesus Christ have received in the New Testament the divine power to bind and to loosen on earth, to remember and to forgive sin with the definite assurance that all this would also be bound or loosened in heaven, remembered or forgiven. And as Christ himself says Matthew 16:19. I will give you the keys of the kingdom of heaven; whatever you bind on earth will be bound in heaven, and whatever you loose on earth will be loosed in heaven. And in John 20:22,23. Receive the Holy Spirit. If you forgive anyone's sins, their sins are forgiven; if you do not forgive them, they are not forgiven. Who will not see in this the great dignity and excellence of the holy ministry?

§ 8. Its excellence is also shown in what Jesus says Matthew 10:40 Anyone who welcomes you welcomes me, and anyone who welcomes me welcomes the one who sent me. Whoever welcomes a prophet as a prophet will receive a prophet's reward, and whoever welcomes a righteous person as a righteous person will receive a righteous person's reward. And if anyone gives even a cup of cold water to one of these little ones who is my disciple, truly I tell you, that person will certainly not lose their reward. Again, in Luke 10:16 it says: Whoever listens to you listens to me; whoever rejects you rejects me; but whoever rejects me rejects him who sent me. With these words, therefore, our dearest Saviour declares how we should honour and fear his ministers and messengers in the holy estate of the clergy.

§ 13. Oh, how cautiously and carefully we need to deal with the true messengers of God so that we are not handed over to God's judgment! How we should love, honour and fear them! We should take them in gladly and listen to them because God values them so highly and they carry out such important and excellent work in the world through which penitence is preached to all men with the offer of the salvation of the souls in Christ Jesus.

§ 14. And oh, how blessed are those who God has found worthy of this holy estate of the clergy and who have been equipped with the necessary talents of the mind. Because, they are concerned with immortal souls and use such powerful words which can captivate the hearts of the listeners to such an extent that they must finally obey God's truth. However, none in the estate of the clergy can lay claim to such divine might, power and glory other than the pious, wise and loyal ministers of the Lord who are united intimately with the omnipotence of the majestic God through their faith and only speak of what Jesus Christ has wrought in them. Romans 15:18.

§ 15. Lastly, the excellence of these faithful ministers also lies in the fact that their work bears everlasting fruit which will bring with it an eternal reward of grace. Because, after the world comes to an end all the works that are of the world will disappear, however exquisite and wonderful they may be. But, because the teachers and preachers are concerned only with immortal souls and eternal goods, all their work which they carried out on the souls of men through untiring teaching, admonition, consolation and punishment will follow them into eternity. Then it will be finally known and revealed how those who have adorned and honoured this estate through a holy and blameless life have considered it to be great and excellent.

THE FOURTH CHAPTER

ABOUT THE IMPORTANCE AND THE RIGOUR OF THE HOLY ESTATE OF THE CLERGY

§ 1. Just as we must believe according to the testimonies of the Holy Scriptures that the estate of the clergy is the most necessary and the best estate in the world, similarly we must also believe that it is also, among all other estates, the most important, the most burdensome and rigorous estate which cannot be entered into without a fearful heart, without worry, toil and work and without a constant watchfulness and struggle to carry it out properly according to the holy will of God and for the salvation of the recalcitrant children of men.

§ 2. All men have been given an immortal soul for which they must care in order that it may be united with its origin. However, those who are in the holy estate of the clergy must care not only for their own souls which they carry in their hands like David. Psalm 119.109, but they also must care for so many hundred other souls which they must lead away from Satan, from sin and from the world to God. They must care not only for those who have been especially entrusted to them and who have submitted themselves to their guidance, but also for all among who they live and with whom they deal and whom they can offer the opportunity to convert.

§ 3. Here, all teachers and preachers should take note of what God the Lord said to the Prophet Ezekiel when he speaks thus in Ezekiel 3:17-19: Son of man, I have made you a watchman for the people of Israel; so hear the word I speak and give them warning from me. When I say to a wicked person, 'You will surely die,' and you do not warn them or speak out to dissuade them from their evil ways in order to save their life, that wicked person will die for their sin, and I will hold you accountable for their blood. But if you do warn the wicked person and they do not turn from their wickedness or from their evil ways, they will die for their sin; but you will have saved yourself. Again, when a righteous person turns from their righteousness and does evil, and I put a stumbling block before them, they will die. Since you did not warn them, they will die for their sin. The righteous things that person did will not be remembered, and I will hold you accountable for their blood. But if you do warn the righteous person not to sin and they do not sin, they will surely live because they took warning, and you will have saved yourself.

§ 4. If then teachers and preachers were to carefully consider this, they would truly not be able to look upon their estate simply as a means to earn a living and seek carnal comfort in it, rather one would find in them a serious concern to save not only their own, but also the souls of their subjects. And, because God knew that many teachers would forget this, he repeated these words once more in Ezekiel 33:1-10 with a parable about a watchman of the country. God did all this not only for the Prophet Ezekiel, who was faithful, but principally also for the sake of those teachers and preachers who would accept this prophet's scripture as God's word, so that they would have a constant reminder of the great importance of their ministry and preside over it in a fitting manner.

§ 5. Now, because teachers and preachers have the care of souls as their work and must always look after them, they will hereafter on that day give a precise account of all the souls entrusted to them in front of the judgement seat of Jesus Christ, their principal shepherd. Paul bears testimony to this when he says Hebrews 13:17: Have confidence in your leaders and submit to their authority, because they keep watch over you as those who must give an account. Do this so that their work will be a joy, not a burden, for that would be of no benefit to you. Certainly, on that day our principal shepherd will not ask us: Were you able to carry out fine disputes in your work and spar well with the warring parties? Were you also able to explain my teachings elegantly according to the rules of logic, metaphysics and rhetoric? Did you get a good income with my ministry of the pastor and other such questions? Oh no! He will ask: Did you lead many souls to me? Were you able to look after the flock entrusted to you? Have you, in all things, saved your conscience, so that even if many thousands were lost to your pastoral ministry they were, nevertheless, sufficiently warned by you, so that it was not yours but their fault that they were lost etc. Oh! Who will not be able to see from this how difficult and important the holy estate of the clergy is!

§ 15. In addition, even a faithful teacher will daily confront many incidental matters in his work so that, if he wishes to have a clear conscience, he will have very few hours of rest or many pleasant days in the world, especially when he considers how the entire kingdom of hell and all the godless in the world are his enemies. They lie in wait for him everywhere and seek to hinder him in all kinds of ways not only in his own Christianity, but also in his work, so that he must always fight against such powerful enemies and no day is without danger.

§ 16. Those who thus wished to enter this holy ministry with the intention of being able to live a peaceful, calm and delightful life, which is what the flesh would like to have, they will find themselves cruelly cheated. Instead of the expected peace there will be agitation and instead of pleasure they will find fear, troubles and heartache if they still have a receptive conscience and have not been completely drawn into the world so that they think neither of their own souls nor of the souls of their listeners. They regard the ministry only as a profession through which one can gain honour, fame, wealth, worldly esteem and carnal comforts. However, even for these hirelings their job can become painful and difficult, indeed more difficult than for the faithful servants. Since the latter do it all from love, therefore, even the most difficult work will become easy. But the former, namely the hirelings, do it all in ill-humour, because they are looking for the wool, not the flock. And when they get the wool, they become lazy and idle so that they are a burden to their listeners and a plague unto themselves.

§ 17. Since this is what the holy estate of the clergy is like one should carefully consider the costs before one wishes to apply oneself to it. And certainly, he who understands its importance will not run after it in supplication, much less in donations, but he will wait till God calls him to it. Even then he will consider all the circumstances and would much rather deny himself a little than to take on such a great and important ministry without reflection, remembering what the holy James said: Not many of you should become teachers, my fellow believers, because you know that we who teach will be judged more strictly. James 3:1.

The Fifth Chapter

About the order in the
Holy Estate of the Clergy

§ 1. God is a God of order. Not only has he created a certain order among his invisible angels in heaven, but he has also instituted a fine order among the children of men on earth in all estates. The ruling estate of the world cannot be managed only by one person. Thus, one finds many and all kinds of persons in it who each have their offices as emperors, kings, electors, princes, privy councilors, counts, governors, authorities and all kinds of employees who all contribute something for the proper support of the ruling estate. In the civil estate also, we find an order among those persons who administer it. Therefore, because the estate of the clergy is superior to the other two it must similarly have a definite order if it is to be maintained properly and the salvation of men is to be carried out properly in accordance with God's will.

§ 5. When the real High Priest and Prophet Christ Jesus came into the world, he found many learned men in the priestly class who could in an elaborate and elegant manner debate about his person, but very few who had converted and would have wanted to recognize and accept him. Therefore, he faced the greatest opposition from the priesthood and had to repeatedly cry out loudly against them. He could not choose any from the estate of the clergy to be his disciples either and instead appointed poor and ignorant fishermen as his disciples. With these he later constituted a completely new estate of the clergy pleasing to him, through which he had his gospel and the doctrine of mercy propagated in the whole world.

§ 6. Meanwhile, although there was no dispute about precedence among the disciples of Christ after the coming of the Holy Spirit with all of them working in the same spirit, the same love and living in a fraternal community, yet a certain order was maintained among them, so that especially James and Cephas and John were considered the pillars. Therefore, although the holy Paul had been called upon by Jesus himself to be an apostle and had been sent among the heathens so that he did not need to be told to do it by the other apostles, he still travelled to Jerusalem to the other twelve apostles in order to be authorized by them to carry out such an important task. He says in Galatians 2:6-9: As for those who were held in high esteem—whatever they were makes no difference to me; God does not show favoritism—they added nothing to my message. On the contrary, they recognized that I had been entrusted with the task of preaching the gospel to the uncircumcised, just as Peter had been to the circumcised. James, Cephas and John, those esteemed as pillars, gave me and Barnabas the right hand of fellowship when they recognized the grace given to me. They agreed that we should go to the Gentiles, and they to the circumcised.

§ 11. Thus, it is a great benefaction of God that such a salutary order of the estate of the clergy has been introduced in the Christian Church, especially since without it there could be no order pleasing to God either in the ruling estate or the civil estate.

And, despite the fact that after many ages through the devil's cunning and because of the insatiable ambition of carnal-minded scholars the high officials of this spiritual estate had risen so high that eventually under the Papacy the spiritual estate had almost become a worldly estate, yet, afterwards our blessed Luther carried out a fine reformation in this and brought everything into good order again. It would, however, be desirable not only to have Luther's good institutions amongst us, but also his spirit, direction and zeal so that whatever Luther began can be continued properly.

§ 12. There are large and small congregations among us; there are universities, also high schools and small schools. There are episcopates, superintendencies and Church councils which must be administered by many people who should be equipped with wisdom, faithfulness and divine zeal, so that through them God can carry out his work in the world and can keep the Christian Church in good order.

§ 13. Therefore, bishops or general superintendents are needed to look after all matters of the Church and not only maintain the quality of the good institutions that have been set up, but also, whenever necessary, to make other edifying arrangements so that through their faithful work the congregation of Christ may be edified in all kinds of ways. It is reasonable, therefore, to obey them in all that they command, organize and carry out according to the rules of the divine word.

§. 14. Loyal officials of the Church Councils, who are in charge especially of the selection of teachers and preachers, are also necessary to ensure that no hirelings and worldly-minded persons but instead pious, wise and godly-minded people are appointed to serve the congregation of Jesus Christ. Watchful inspectors are also necessary. They constantly examine all the congregations and pay attention to the teachings and to the lives of the teachers and preachers, since one always wishes to know whether one has a hireling or a faithful teacher as one's shepherd. The inspectors are also necessary to promote the latter in their faith and to either cleanse the former of their attitude as hirelings or to dismiss them from the job entirely.

§ 15. In addition, faithful and hardworking professors are needed in universities who can guide the students of theology properly in the Holy Scriptures and give them the best aids for a thorough understanding of the Holy Scriptures so that they do not become Aristotelian or Platonic theologians, but rather prophetic and apostolic theologians who can later oversee the congregation of Jesus Christ with wisdom, faith and honesty.

§ 16. Capable teachers and preachers are also necessary who can communicate the word of truth properly and who insist on an upright Christianity in all their teaching and preaching. Under them it is especially necessary to have experienced catechists who know how to teach the youth the fundamentals of the Christian doctrine in a light and easy manner and who can, therefore, present and explain Christianity, even the most difficult parts of the Holy Scriptures, with simple questions.

THE SIXTH CHAPTER

ABOUT THE DIFFERENCE BETWEEN
THE MINISTRY AND SPIRITUAL PRIESTHOOD

§ 1. We can show from both the Old and the New Testament that apart from the regular estate of the clergy there is also a general ecclesiastic priesthood which concerns all Christians and should be practiced by all as is shown both in the Old and in the New Testament. In the Old Testament God himself says to the people of Israel: Now if you obey me fully and keep my covenant, then out of all nations you will be my treasured possession. Although the whole earth is mine, you will be for me a kingdom of priests and a holy nation. Exodus 19:5,6. And in the Prophet Isaiah 61:6 it says: And you will be called priests of the LORD, you will be named ministers of our God.

§ 2. In the New Testament this is declared more grandly when it says 1 Peter 2:5: You also, like living stones, are being built into a spiritual house to be a holy priesthood, offering spiritual sacrifices acceptable to God through Jesus Christ. And in the following verses Peter says: But you are a chosen people, a royal priesthood, a holy nation, God's special possession, that you may declare the praises of him who called you out of darkness into his wonderful light. Similarly, in the revelation of John (Revelation 1:6): And has made us to be a kingdom and priests to serve his God and Father, which is praised again in the following Chapter 5:10 by the twenty-four elders.

§ 3. However, the regular ministry is quite different from the spiritual priesthood as we see in Numbers 8:6 that although all Israelites were spiritual priests, God still commanded that the Levites should be taken from among all the other children of Israel and dedicated as his special possession. Therefore, it would be wrong if we who are all spiritual priests were to dissolve the regular estate of the clergy completely or despise it. The difference between the two, however, can be seen from the following.

§ 4. The spiritual priesthood requires that one is anointed by him who is holy and knows everything 1 John 2:20, so that one can always be prepared and be responsible for giving everyone the reason for the hope that is in us, but with gentleness and respect. 1 Peter 3:15,16. But the regular ministry demands a far greater and more complete study and knowledge of all those truths that are written in God's word; in order that these can be presented to everyone with far greater authority and more important evidence according to God's economy.

§ 5. The spiritual priesthood requires that one help one another, each using whatever gift he has received as faithful stewards of the various forms of God's grace. 1 Peter 4:10. But the regular ministry of the preacher requires far more and greater gifts, to be used both orally and in writing in a salutary and edifying manner for the benefit of God's congregation and with a view to multiplying it so abundantly that such a teacher may one day hear the joyful voice say: Well done, good and faithful servant. You have been faithful with a few things; I will put you in charge of many things. Come and share your master's happiness. Matthew 25:21.

§ 10. Even though every Christian, on the strength of his spiritual priesthood, is bound to both observe God's word himself as well as to act with others, yet the dealing of this holy word is entrusted to the regular ministry in a special way. These teachers must not only act on it in private with others on all appropriate occasions, but they are also duty-bound to explain and teach it publicly in churches and schools which requires a far greater capability than the former action. And, in order that no one on account of the spiritual priesthood despises the public ministry or interferes with it, the holy Paul writes in a considered manner in the 14th Chapter of his first epistle to the Corinthians, verse 32, 33 and 34: The spirits of the prophets are subject to the control of prophets. For God is not a God of disorder but of peace—as in all the congregations of the Lord's people.

§ 11. As far as the spiritual priesthood is concerned, even women are bound to become good teachers Titus 2:3 as we read in the Acts 18:2.26 about how the pious Priscilla invited the learned Apollos to her home and explained to him the way of God in a better manner. Thus, we also read in the following chapter Acts 21:8,9 about the evangelist Philip that he had four unmarried daughters who prophesied. But, as far as the public ministry of the preacher is concerned Paul writes about women in 1 Timothy 2:11,12: A woman should learn in quietness and full submission. I do not permit a woman to teach or to assume authority over a man; she must be quiet. And, in 1 Corinthians 14:34: Women should remain silent in the churches. They are not allowed to speak, but must be in submission, as the law also says.

§ 12. The spiritual priesthood also concerns all kings and worldly regents who are bound to exhort, to warn and to punish their subjects and also to pray for them as we can see in the example of the wise king Solomon who, when the temple was being consecrated, stood among the people and not only blessed the whole assembly of Israel, but also stood before the altar of the Lord in front of the whole assembly of Israel, spread out his hands toward heaven and, in the presence of all the people, spoke a long and moving prayer. 1 Kings 8:12.

§ 14. Even if it is clear from the above that kings, princes and potentates too, on account of the spiritual priesthood, can teach, exhort, console and bless their subjects when the occasion arises, this duty has been enjoined far more seriously on those who are in the public estate of the clergy. They also have a special calling to it, and, in this regard, they have a great authority. They are looked upon as messengers and ambassadors of God, which is why even kings, princes and potentates, taking this into consideration, allow themselves to be taught, consoled and exhorted by them as if by God himself.

§ 15. Moreover, worldly regents would not presume to teach publicly from the pulpits. Because, even if King Solomon was a preacher at Jerusalem, Ecclesiastes 1:12, he only preached on Mount Zion in his royal residence, never in the temple without being ordained by it. And, although he wrote many beautiful proverbs and excellent teachings, he did not in any way impede the estate of the clergy, rather he graced and promoted them in this way, so that even today all teachers and preachers have a lot to thank him for because of his wise proverbs and edifying teachings.

§ 20. Therefore, neither should spiritual priesthood be invalidated and hindered because of the regular estate of the clergy, nor should this estate be invalidated and hindered because of spiritual priesthood. Rather, all listeners in the worldly and civil estate should honour and value the estate of the clergy, and all priests and preachers should recommend that their listeners honour the spiritual priesthood and exercise it in the best way possible. Thus, in deed and in truth the priests and preachers testify that they are not ashamed to allow themselves to be exhorted and reminded by other spiritual priests.

THE SEVENTH CHAPTER

ABOUT THE GRAVE DETERIORATION OF THE PRESENT ESTATE OF THE CLERGY

§ 1. The holy estate of the clergy is a necessary, excellent and glorious estate in the world for all men to achieve true wisdom and bliss through which the kingdom of the devil can be destroyed, and the kingdom of God can be established. It is also, among the estates, the one that always has been most troubled by the devil and brought into all kinds of disarray so that one has erred both in the clarity of the doctrine or in its well-founded presentation as well as in the sanctity of life. The devil well knows that if he can establish his rule in this estate through mischievous sins, he can easily keep all the other estates in disarray and in sin to serve him.

§ 2. Therefore, because even today the devil has brought in such a grave deterioration into the estate of the clergy through his many tricks, even tears are not enough to lament this. It is, however, necessary, according to the testimony of the Holy Scriptures, to reveal such deterioration with compassionate love in the hope that there will still be some who will allow themselves to be moved by this and will strive in all seriousness and zeal to remedy such deterioration through combined effort and to set everything right again.

§ 7. See, this is what is happening in the estate of the clergy even today! All teachers and preachers should be scouts of the promised land of future bliss, they should have gone down all its paths and acquired proper knowledge about the merciful kingdom of Jesus Christ and of the kingdom of glory. Only then can they not only show their congregations the correct path to it and talk about its real nature, but through exhortation and encouragement they can imbue them with cheerful courage, so that even if they are subjected to many afflictions on this path and have to conquer high mountains it would not be impossible to overcome all this and, through many struggles, achieve the promised land of bliss. But, just as those scouts made the people anxious about the impossibility, these also do the same. They say: We cannot teach and live as the prophets, Christ and the holy apostles did, we cannot do what we ourselves teach and preach. We cannot walk the narrow path that God's word prescribes. We can only hope that Christ gives us this promised land out of mercy without our making such great efforts to achieve it. In this way even those who had begun to struggle for heaven are deterred from their good intentions and everyone excuses himself with its impossibility. Even if a Caleb were to appear and, through God's word, bear testimony to its possibility, he would not be heard.

§ 8. In Numbers 16:1-3 the priests and Levites themselves revolted against Moses and Aaron and said to them: You have gone too far! The whole community is holy, every one of them, and the LORD is with them. Why then do you set yourselves above the LORD's assembly? Even today such opposition often arises among the teachers and preachers because when some, out of divine motives, declaim passionately against the godless nature of Christians and refuse to be satisfied either with the hypocritical pretenders or with the opere operato (the proper discharge especially of the sacraments), but insist instead on the exercise of an active and upright Christianity while demonstrating it themselves in their deeds and their life, see: immediately carnal-minded teachers stand up and rise against such faithful workers accusing them of insisting too much on good works and drawing the bow too tight when everything was actually in a good condition and the status Ecclesiae florentissimus (status of a flourishing Church) was prevalent.

§ 16. In the 8th Chapter of the Prophet Isaiah we hear such people chattering and debating. Ah! if this holy prophet should visit our schools, universities and churches today he would find such a great deal of chattering and debating in them that his bloody tears would not be enough to bemoan such heathen behavior. Where are the Holy Scriptures dealt with properly today in schools and universities? Hasn't one instead introduced the writings of Aristoteles, long in hell, and other heathen texts so that the doctrine of Jesus Christ about faith and love has become a pernicious art of quarrels, squabbles and debates? And, because one has been mainly taught this in schools and universities and one has not been concerned with faith and love, one sees that later in the pulpit one is better in debating with absent, contentious parties than in speaking to those present about faith and love.

§ 19. About such teachers and preachers, the Prophet Isaiah writes in the following chapter, Isaiah 29:21: Those who with a word make someone out to be guilty, who ensnare the defender in court and with false testimony deprive the innocent of justice. Oh, dear one, how can it happen that people can be made to sin through preaching? There are no proofs necessary for this, because our daily experience teaches it: especially since such carnal-minded teachers like to claim that they are pious and holy preachers pleasing to God. However, because the listeners see so many vices and bad habits in them, they cover them up and, in their sermons, take great pains to draw on only those passages which deal with human misery. But they ignore those passages that deal with revival, sanctification and preparation for the divine image or only explain them in their carnal way. Therefore, the people are made secure and presume that they have been converted and are a loving people of God. They also cry out loud: God is pleased with us, now there is lasting peace, all quarrels have now ended. Thus, each one remains as he was as a youth and becomes even worse. This, therefore, means that they make people sin through their preaching.

§ 24. If one examines the condition of scholars today in the light of these words one finds that what happened in the times of Jeremiah is also happening among them; it is important, therefore, that we have the enlightened eyes of the prophet and his spirit. One finds a lot of teaching done in schools, universities and in churches, but it is usually only hay, straw and stubble and nothing good that could give strength and nourishment for the immortal soul. However, one still presumes on the Holy Scriptures and wants to be respected as if one were a great admirer of these Scriptures, whereas one rejects the word of God and refuses to be satisfied with its simplicity, purity and clarity. Instead, it is subjected to the examination of heathen philosophy and must allow itself to be judged, explained and turned around by it to the best advantage of the carnal-minded person. But one is not allowed to say this to them or to write about it, because they do not want to be disgraced and feel any shame. They say if one were to do this, their ministry would be maligned and dishonoured, not seeing that they themselves disgrace and dishonor the same and, therefore, deserve to be disgraced and dishonoured. This would be for their good, so that from now on they would learn to honour God's word better and would try to embellish it with a holy life so that it would have greater authority among the common people.

§ 28. The Prophet Jeremiah says the following about such carnal-minded shepherds and teachers in Jeremiah 10:21: The shepherds are senseless and do not inquire of the LORD; so they do not prosper and all their flock is scattered. One also finds this among many of the shepherds and teachers today. One sees that some of them are so enamoured of heathen philosophy that they expend ten times more effort in learning the subtleties of logic, metaphysics and rhetoric than in learning the Holy Scriptures. And, because their brain is filled with such clatter they later want to deal with the holy word of God in speech and writing only according to the rules of such heathen philosophy. Therefore, God makes them fools in their art, and such fools that they cannot even recognise their own foolishness, wanting to sell it as great wisdom. But earnest theologians, well-versed in God, see such foolishness and realise that it is so completely opposed to their own gravity that they should not defile themselves with such heathen things. And, even if they are great lovers of pure philosophy, they learn it not from heathen books but from the book of nature and from themselves in the divine light by becoming one with him who created all natural things.

§ 29. Through these wrong shepherds and teachers, it is not the kingdom of Christ but the kingdom of Aristoteles that grows and increases, and the vineyard they were meant to take care of and cultivate, they instead ruin and destroy. Therefore, God complains about them to the Prophet Jeremiah when he says: Many shepherds will ruin my vineyard and trample down my field; they will turn my pleasant field into a desolate wasteland. It will be made a wasteland, parched and desolate before me; the whole land will be laid waste because there is no one who cares. Jeremiah 12:11. Assuredly, those whose eyes have been opened by God to see the great harm and damage brought into the Christian Church by such wrong teachers, they will surely not take it amiss that, with a deep sigh, I must write so strongly against them from the heartfelt desire to see Christ's vineyard cleansed of such evil workers and henceforth occupied only by faithful workers.

§ 30. O, how the pious prophet was moved to sigh when he saw the immense damage caused to the people of Israel by the false prophets when he says: Alas, Sovereign LORD! The prophets keep telling them, you will not see the sword or suffer famine. Indeed, I will give you lasting peace in this place. Then the LORD said to me, "The prophets are prophesying lies in my name. I have not sent them or appointed them or spoken to them. They are prophesying to you false visions, divinations, idolatries and the delusions of their own minds. Jeremiah 14:13,14. We know that at that time such false prophets among the people of Israel were proper teachers and preachers who had, since their youth, studied the laws and other sciences and had also been appointed to their ministry by other men. Yet, God says, he had not appointed them because they were outside his community and through their unholy life slandered his name not only themselves but also misled the people into a false sense of security and a constant opposition to the faithful prophets. One finds many such people today in the estate of the clergy who have studied at schools and universities and acquired a pedantic knowledge of theology and have later been appointed to public ministries through their good friends and patrons. But, nevertheless, because they did not allow themselves to be also taught, converted, enlightened, sanctified and appointed by God they are merely self-appointed prophets with whom God is not associated. Therefore, they will only turn a thousand souls the wrong way and not convert even one soul.

§ 47. In the meanwhile, however, the grave deterioration of the estate of the clergy in all its facets has not been described fully for it is so grave that not one, but many books can be written about it. I only wanted to provide an opportunity for more reflection on the matter so that with the passages quoted from the Scriptures the present condition of teachers and preachers is examined carefully. I bear witness before God, however, that I have not written this out of carnal emotions, but out of compassionate love and with many tears hoping that in consideration of the distress that I suffer for the sake of the truth my zeal is not taken amiss, rather one prays that this zeal is increased.

§ 48. It is not my intention to provide an opportunity to despise the holy ministry; rather one is trying to free it from the contempt it has been held in hitherto. Because, after such a holy ministry has been damaged and dishonoured by the ungodly life and by the carnal-minded scholastics of the worldly preachers it cannot be freed from its dishonour and achieve its proper honour unless teachers and preachers now begin to change both their life and their sterile manner of teaching and instead orient themselves only to the rules of the divine word. Besides, although the deterioration is great, I know that here and there some honest teachers and preachers are to be found who will not feel insulted by this but who will try to find ways to demonstrate to the hirelings more clearly and in greater detail what I have written here briefly for greater reflection and in order to see whether there are perhaps many more who will follow us and work faithfully to propagate the merciful kingdom of Jesus Christ.

The Second Part of The Estate of The Clergy Pleasing to God (abridged)

With instructions on how one can achieve a proper proficiency in it

The First Chapter

How one should apply oneself to piety from one's youth and organize one's studies befittingly

§ 1. If a person wants to apply himself to a craft or a trade, he first tends to estimate the cost and reflects on it for some time on his own: how do matters stand with this craft or trade, what profits as well as what efforts and troubles are to be expected from it, as also how can it be learnt best? Then, after he has weighed all the conditions and has explored the strength of his body and mind, and if he concludes that he will find his purpose in it regardless of the fact that it will cost him much effort and work, he sets about the work joyfully, continues and perseveres in it even if it often seems quite difficult, because he already knew in the beginning that it would be difficult and troublesome. On the other hand, he would be very double-minded if he had imagined it to be easy or if he had not thought about it at all.

§ 2. If this is carried out in lowly matters by the children of men, then it is indeed necessary to follow it assiduously in higher matters that concern the soul and the eternal. In the world there is no higher and more important profession one can apply oneself to than holy theology or the study of theology. Therefore, before one sets one's mind on it, he has good reason to ponder over it. How do matters stand with this holy study and what kind of person should one be if one wanted to do it, as also what efforts and work are required to learn this and what dangers, burdens and difficult challenges will it give rise to if one wants to work conscientiously? If a person weighs all these considerations properly, he will progress well in this study and he will not allow himself to be deterred from it when he sees that he will not only have a lot of trouble, but that he will also be tested severely.

§ 3. But, a person who imagines such a study of theology as promising only good days and who looks on it as an opportunity to acquire a carnal good life, comforts, great honour and wealth, he will either change his plans and fall back on other studies when he sees that it entails so many difficulties and such a great renunciation of the world and of one's self, or he will gradually lose the sensitivity of his conscience and, with other carnal-minded theologians he will go into it at random without thinking about the account he will have to give of it hereafter.

§ 4. Theology is concerned with the triune God and with divine, heavenly, spiritual and eternal matters. Therefore, it also requires a mind that is attuned to the divine, the heavenly and the spiritual and that directs its attention only towards the eternal, the hereafter and the imperceptible. Such a mind can understand that theology alone is divine, heavenly and spiritual, while the normal man does not perceive anything of God's spirit. The person without the Spirit does not accept the things that come from the Spirit of God but considers them foolishness and cannot understand them because they are discerned only through the Spirit. 1 Corinthians 2:14. If then an ordinary or unenlightened theologian always deals immediately with spiritual and divine truths and also has a fairly pedantic understanding of them, he only perceives them in a worldly, material and ordinary manner and never in the way they should be perceived, namely in a heavenly, spiritual and divine way so that they are also felt, tasted, enjoyed and exercised in the soul.

§ 5. Therefore, it is necessary that, above all, one should try to attain a position where God is pleased with an enthusiast of this holy study, and through a devout union can enlighten, teach, sanctify and favour him with true wisdom, also help him in all his work and enable the desired progress in his purpose. If one is in such a position of grace even the most difficult work will become easy and everything will proceed with rich blessings. If, however, a person does not wish to attain such a position he will not only be robbed of all of God's blessings, but he will also never be able to achieve a living knowledge of divine truths with the natural powers of his soul, nor will he achieve proper theological proficiency.

§ 6. However, if one is to attain such a blessed position of grace all the powers of his soul and his heart must undergo a great change. Because, after the deplorable fall from grace man is completely depraved and unfit for the company of God. The will is wrong and completely opposed to the will of God. Reason is eclipsed and far more suited to accepting erroneous ideas than to accepting those truths that should be exercised by the will. All thoughts, desires, feelings and all emotions and stirrings of the heart are in great confusion. From all this there arises a very bad and sinful use of the external senses. Therefore, it is necessary that the heart and the mind undergo a salutary change so that the whole man with the powers of his body and soul can be made dependent on God again through true conversion.

§ 7. Most people allow themselves to be stopped from such conversion and want to postpone it till such time as they enter public ministry. Therefore, one sees that those who choose theology, both in schools and in universities, lead a very worldly life in all kinds of debauchery and sensual exuberance saying that they would soon enough have to adopt a tiresome monastic life where they would be compelled to forgo cheerful social gatherings and lead a quiet life in their black caps. In their youth then they are ministers of the devil while pursuing this holy study and after that the black cap is meant to make them ministers of God. I fear, however, that those who in their youth and in their school-years have not honestly converted to God will then hardly be converted through their ministry. Because, even though they cannot any longer lead such a shameless and openly godless life to keep up appearances before the world, their hearts remain unchanged and they end up in hypocrisy from which it is far more difficult to convert them than when they were living in open disgrace and depravity.

§ 8. If, therefore, a person wants to escape such traps of the devil and become a theologian pleasing to God he has reason to convert to God early while still in his tender youth and make serious efforts to become a pleasing child of God and a well-prepared vessel for the Holy Spirit. To this end he must search out the companionship of pious souls and see whether he can get a person who is experienced, wise and well-practiced in the ways of God as his guide and mentor, with whom he can always talk and from whom he can get good advice if Satan or the world wishes to hinder him in his work.

§ 9. However, he must not depend only on the guidance of such persons, he must also get to know our dear God properly through constant prayer, supplication and sighs. He must begin to examine himself in the light of God's word to see how he is doing, how he should grow and further increase in goodness, and how and in which way the pleasures of youth and of all worldly temptations can be denied through God's strength. Along with this he must also lead a quiet and withdrawn life, detached from the world so that God and heavenly wisdom can work on him and bring his mind to such a disposition and harmony that in future he can grasp, understand, recognize, remember and practise everything that he must deal with.

§ 10. If a person has come this far, he should then organize his studies properly as pious and experienced men see fit and as rendered necessary by his condition. Above all, he must reflect on why he is in the world and why he wishes to study theology. His reasons should not be to become a highly-learned man who should be extolled, honoured, praised, loved by all men and elevated to positions of high dignity, but his purpose should only be that this holy study may enlighten and sanctify his soul to achieve the lost divine image. Also, that it should make him capable of promoting the honour of his God, of extending His kingdom, propagating the divine truth and of seeking and maintaining in all seriousness the salvation of his fellow-men and his own welfare.

§ 11. It is true that with this holy purpose a lover of divine theology will encounter many hindrances and difficulties. However, if he tries seriously and exercises piety daily, he will, with patience and

God's help, overcome everything and achieve his final purpose. In this he must remember that all men are born for trouble and work. Also, how it is an uncommonly great benefaction that God has chosen him for such work in this world which leads to a constant improvement of souls and deals only with such matters that are true, constant, divine, spiritual and eternal. Therefore, it would also bear true, constant, divine, spiritual and eternal fruit from which eternal reward will follow. This way of thinking will be able to cheer him up, especially when he considers how other people often have far greater work and troubles for which they can get nothing more than their material sustenance.

§ 12. If then a student of theology has a proper and firm purpose in mind, he must also organize all his studies according to this so that he is not gradually led away from his purpose unintentionally. He must explore the nature of his talent and the strength of his body. He must consider how the Genera Studiorum (subjects of study) are many, but the years of our life are very few. Therefore, one must choose the most necessary and useful ones which will lead most closely to the goal. Because it is far better to choose only a few subjects to which one is driven most by God and by one's heart and to qualify well in these rather than to want to study all subjects and not gain proper solidity in any.

§ 13. Among the subjects of humanistic studies, the most necessary and useful is the study of languages which should be started and continued properly if one is not to lose too much time with it and hindered in other subjects. Here it would be necessary to be directed towards learning words from a tender age and being spared the memorizing of extensive grammars. This would help one achieve one's purpose better and, later, when reading the authors one can, with a little effort also learn all grammatical rules. This is what I have experienced here in learning the Malabarian language which I learnt without grammatical instructions so well in one year through reading, listening and speaking that I could not only catechize and preach extempore in it every day, but I could later also write a proper dictionary and grammar. In Europe I had to spend more than 12 years learning Latin, Greek and Hebrew. With instructions from a wise and true preceptor one can save a lot of time in this.

§ 14. One should not, however, look at languages as wisdom and erudition in themselves, falsely thinking that one is a wise and knowledgeable theologian if one understands and can speak all kinds of languages. Rather, one should regard them as instruments to acquire true wisdom as well as to communicate this acquired wisdom to other nations and languages. Therefore, just as someone is not a musician if he has bought all kinds of musical instruments, if he cannot also play them harmoniously and thus inspire himself and others to praise God, similarly a person who has learnt many languages cannot immediately be considered a theologian and a wise man if in his heart he did not feel that he could advance himself and others to true wisdom through the languages he had learnt. In consideration of this a person would remain humble even if he were trained in many languages and were to be praised for it by many people.

§ 15. Besides the study of languages, the study of physics is a pleasure and delight and it can be paired well with the study of theology. Here, however, one should not allow oneself to be led astray by the Aristotelians and be plagued by ordinary physical science. Because in learning that one would lose rather than gain reason. God himself has written an open and clear physics for us in his creatures, and to learn this the instructions of Aristoteles with their intricate terms are not at all necessary. If one observes all visible things carefully in God's light and ponders over their origin, their being, their qualities, effects and manifold uses, one would be able to study the best kind of physics and would become one with divine miracles. If one were to try and bring together the book of nature and the Holy Scriptures, then such a study of physics will be a big aid in the study of theology and give rise to joy and pleasure for its admirer, so that he will be able to use all of God's creatures for their correct purpose and thus learn to understand many divine secrets in the Holy Scriptures.

§ 16. As far as ethics is concerned one can learn it far more easily and more productively from the wise proverbs of Solomon, from the Sirach and from the epistles of Paul rather than from the books of Aristotelian philosophers. Because, the latter often ignore the best virtues, do not provide any proper foundation or the means to avoid vices and to practise virtues daily. Therefore, when one looks at the lives of such moral philosophers one finds only hypocrisy and vices and thus their moral teachings are found to be only an empty and powerless idea in the brain. Undoubtedly, it is a great insult to God's word that we as Christians ignore it in the improvement of our souls and nurture the foolish idea that the speculations of learned heathens or of contemporary philosophers can give us greater strength in the practise of virtues and better instruction about our souls than through the holy word of God that has been revealed to us. A person who is, therefore, willing to be advised, should choose the Holy Scriptures as his ethics and earnestly try to know himself thoroughly. In this way he will also notice great progress in his study of theology.

§ 17. I would not want to recommend a study of logic and metaphysics to any admirer of pure theology because of the way that it is dealt with today in most schools, especially since not only is a lot of time wasted with it, but also because where it has captured the heart it causes so much damage in theology that tears are not enough to bemoan this. Since men by nature tend to quarrel and fight, these disciplines are a pure poison through which our inborn incivility can come into prominence in subtle debates against our fellow-men, in which the desire to titillate means that one can overturn the most certain truths and make lies into truths. Once one has become accustomed to this one later uses such disciplines in all theological matters and deals with the holy word of God in a shameless, carnal and worldly manner. This can only bring calamity, damage and a curse on the Christian Church.

§ 18. In the light of this an admirer of theology should take note of Paul's advice to the young Timothy when he says: Timothy, guard what has been entrusted to your care. Turn away from godless chatter and the opposing ideas of what is falsely called knowledge, which some have professed and in so doing have departed from the faith. 1 Timothy 6:20,21. However, if someone is in such a school where such disciplines are taught, which he cannot change, he may also listen to them in order to understand their foolishness, but he must be careful not to learn them in order to use them later in theology. Because that would be his ruin and would hinder the good in him.

§ 19. As far as rhetoric and oratory are concerned, they are like logic and metaphysics and should rather be avoided than learnt. I can give an assurance that if a person has a proper knowledge and a living experience of spiritual and natural things, he will be able to speak about them quite clearly, properly and in an edifying manner without the help of the rules of oratory. But if he does not have a proper understanding of a thing nor the proper experience it would be a torture for him to compose a speech according to the prescribed rules of oratory. The study of this should, therefore, be left to those who have no experience and practise in theological truths and who only mean to become hypocritical liars who have a stigma on their conscience and try to lead innocent hearts astray with sweet words and brilliant speeches. 1 Timothy 4:2; Romans 16:18. But, those who in days to come mean to serve God honestly in their ministry and to edify their fellow-men with the simplicity of the divine word, they should only work hard to understand and practise the divine truths and they will later be told what, how, where and to whom they should speak and write.

§ 20. The study of history is, as of now, the most delightful and is not only useful and pleasant in ordinary life but is also very beneficial to the study of theology. However, one should not go into it extensively before one has achieved maturity in other more necessary subjects. One should also study it as a subject of secondary importance till one can form a proper opinion, because after that the same can be completed in a short time, namely insofar as it may be necessary for a student of theology. The study of history can be accompanied by the study of geography, which is also useful. In younger years, however, arithmetic should be studied properly because it sharpens mental judgement and teaches it students patient reflection.

§ 21. However, a lover of theology should not allow himself to be held up too long by such studies and should not think that he should not take up a study of theology till such time as he has learnt all the subjects of humanistic studies properly. Rather, he should only look at all of them with the left eye, but the study of theology with the right eye and he should deal with the former in such a way that they promote his study of theology rather than become a hindrance to it. However, he will make mistakes in all this and do too much of something or too little unless he has a true and well-experienced preceptor who knows how to direct him according to his talent.

§ 22. If one wants to study mainly theology one must allow the study of the Bible to be recommended above everything else, because without it nothing solid can be achieved in theology. Besides the diligent reading and contemplation of the divine word one should choose a book in which the entire thetical theology is presented clearly, purely and in an apostolic manner without the use of philosophical terms, such as Herr Dr. Lütken's *Erkenntnis der Wahrheit zur Gottseligkeit* or Herr Dr. Spener's *Sciographia Sacra Articulorum Fidei* or Herr Freylinghausen's *Grundlegung der Theologie*. One should study such books by oneself, refer diligently to the Loca Scripturae and from the order of the articles of faith learn to recognise God's great economy in the salvation of our souls.

§ 23. If a person has made himself familiar with such a book along with the Holy Scriptures, then he can, while repeatedly reading these, also read other theological books at the same time, especially on Sundays when he, in any case, should contemplate purely spiritual matters. However, he should choose such books which lead him closest to the Holy Scriptures and make him devote himself even more to true piety. For this he again needs the advice of a pious and wise theologian who will show him the difference between the necessary and the unnecessary, the useful and the useless, edifying and unedifying books, so that by reading all kinds of books he does not thwart his soul and fall prey to only such knowledge that inflates rather than improving it.

§ 24. Once one has gained a good familiarity with theology in theory and practise it will be easy for him to also familiarize himself with the antithesis. Because, if a person knows for certain which is the correct path and walks this path, he also knows the path that he should not take, especially since, apart from the true path on which he is, all others must be either false or be a detour. On the other hand, even if someone were to know all the detours and the false paths it does not mean that he knows the correct path. Similarly, if one were to know all the antitheses from polemical theology it does not follow that he is conversant with all the theses. Therefore, it is very wrong to study polemical theology before one has gained a good foundation in thetical theology. But only such people do this who generally have studied logic and metaphysics in schools. In polemical theology they then find good arguments for their old Adam in order to display their philosophical skills through constant debates pro and contra. In thetical theology, on the contrary, when it is dealt with properly, they are directed only towards practise, which their old Adam does not approve of.

§ 25. The study of homiletics should be helpful for a student of theology provided it is done properly according to God's word and properly presents the duties and virtues of a preacher. But, in the way it is generally dealt with today in universities it only points out to the rules and precepts with which one can, even without any experience, deal with spiritual matters and preach to ordinary people not from the innermost feelings of the heart but rather from the brain. This is more harmful than productive for the final purpose of the theologian. Even if a contemporary preacher has come far, he still only knows how to deliver sermons that are artificial, seek favours and are full of vapour, which lead to damage rather than edification.

§ 26. If a person wants to do well in theology, he should apply himself diligently to a study of exegetics. But very few universities will offer him a proper opportunity for this. And even if such lectures are held, one tries to make such a study so extensive and annoying for the listeners that most of the students only learn the rules and some other minor subtleties. But the matter itself is never taken up properly. Instead of embarking on such extensive digressions I would rather advise that some pious students who have already gained some understanding of the truth of piety come together and carry out an exegesis of one of the evangelists or of an epistle of Paul while constantly applying it to themselves. This exercise, even if it seems a bit difficult in the beginning, will gradually become quite easy and will also enable one to speak sincerely.

§ 27. A catechetical study should be carried out diligently by a student of theology as it will be of great use afterwards for one's work. A person who has diligently practised this achieves a proper clarity so that he can present even the most difficult matter and the deepest secrets in a simple, clear and thorough manner. But even though such a study is necessary and useful one finds very few and very poor institutions for this. Therefore, one sees that some theologians are good orators and well-practised preachers, but if they have to formulate questions with the children beyond the established questions for catechism and have to catechise extempore on a matter it is dry and is neither edifying, tasteful nor pleasant. Thus, their catechumen have to torture themselves by memorising difficult and long questions which are not made clear or comprehensible to them through simpler and shorter questions. The reason why they have so little practise in this is because catechisation requires much more experience than preaching, which today has become an art so that even the most godless can preach. But catechisation can be done in an edifying and proper manner only by those who have theology not only in their brains but also in their hearts.

§ 28. If a person, therefore, wishes to undertake this study he should not wait till a series of lectures is held in universities or till he is in public ministry, rather he should look for such opportunities even in his school-years. He should ask Christian parents to allow him to catechise their children twice or three times a week. He should do it first with very short and simple questions he has formulated himself so that the children never have to learn more than one or two small passages which he will use to catechise them. In this way the children will never find such teaching tiresome and will always enjoy listening to the questions and replying to them in their innocent manner, even if it is with a simple yes or no. Certainly, the benefit that the children receive from this is indescribable, and the person who has practised like this with them will later find that such an exercise has given him an advantage in theology whose worth cannot be sufficiently weighed in gold.

§ 29. In this, and in all other studies, it should be noted that a lover of true theology need never depend only on his own strengths and skills but should always submit himself to God and appeal to him for wisdom, reason and intelligence. This should not be done as a routine matter but from the innermost core of his heart. Therefore, it is also necessary that he becomes accustomed from his youth to pray in his own words from his heart. This will not only bring him the strength and grace of God, but it will also teach him to speak to people earnestly about spiritual matters. It is also important to observe here that one should neither allow all this study to divert him from his main purpose, nor should one fall prey to empty knowledge. Rather, one should remain all the time in true piety and allow knowledge to gain a proper maturity through its constant practise.

THE SECOND CHAPTER

HOW ONE SHOULD STRIVE AFTER TRUE WISDOM IN THE STUDY OF THEOLOGY

§ 1. True wisdom is very necessary for all people in the world if one wishes to be released from one's general misery and deep deterioration and placed in a state of God's grace in which one is not only pleasing to the triune God and can partake of his blessing in time and eternity, but one also knows how to use God's creatures properly, so that the well-being of our soul and our body is promoted. Therefore, it also says in the Book of Wisdom, Chapter 7[2] that those who acquire wisdom win God's friendship. And the wise king Solomon said: Wisdom, like an inheritance, is a good thing and benefits those who see the sun. Ecclesiastes 7:11. Thus, if one does not have it, one will not find any true pleasure in the world; instead, everything one deals with will only cause anxiety, misery of the heart and, afterwards, also an eternal punishment if we do not save ourselves from it in time.

---

[2] Cf. The Wisdom Chapters. URL: https://www.catholic.org/bible/book. php?id=27&bible (last access: 18 March 2019). All passages from the Wisdom Chapters are taken from this source.

§ 2. If true wisdom is necessary for all men for the use of spiritual and natural things, then one may certainly believe that it is far more necessary for a student of theology, especially since he has to deal with divine secrets and heavenly things which require not only a divine light and heavenly enlightenment of reason, but also an honesty or sincerity and sanctity of will. One needs this if one is to perceive divine secrets in the full conviction of one's heart and if one has to introduce and deal with them properly afterwards to honour God and for the salvation of men.

§ 3. When one hears of wisdom, however, one immediately has a false notion of it and thinks of a wisdom that was introduced into Christianity from heathenism to the detriment of many people, for it is only concerned with a false improvement of the mind without any guidance for a thorough change of will. Therefore, those people who begin to acquire such wisdom normally stop being good Christians. Those who wish to understand such people and be on guard against them will find enough guidance for it in my *Allgemeine Schule der wahren Weisheit* and will see true wisdom painted in lively colours through the wonderful testimonials of the Holy Scriptures.

§ 4. A student of theology should not, therefore, allow himself to be discouraged when he hears everywhere from the worldly scholars and reads in many books that logic and metaphysics are the key to wisdom, without which one cannot reach the hidden depths of wisdom and erudition. If he places his faith in God instead of in such liars, he can truly reach true wisdom much faster than the students of worldly erudition can achieve knowledge of their key. Because it is a strange key which closes rather than opens God's secrets both in nature as well as in the Holy Scriptures. Thus, it is an extreme foolishness that so many people buy such a key at such a high cost, sacrificing the strength of body and soul in order to have nothing more in their reason and their brain than only the key to natural and divine truths. This key they then try to sell at the same price as it has cost them and, in this way, only the key circulates among such worldly-wise people and neither the seller nor the buyer can open the door to true wisdom with it. This is a just punishment for all those who have left the fountain of truth and seek to quench their thirst in the dirty puddles of heathen texts.

§ 14. In schools and universities there is so much fuss made about the doctrine of rationalism by learning which one tries to arrive at a clear mind that can reflect properly about all things and can communicate it in speech clearly and systematically to others. If, however, a student was to apply himself diligently only to true wisdom he would attain this talent much earlier and with far less effort from God rather than from the doctrine of rationalism. Its student says: And so, I prayed, and understanding was given me; I entreated, and the spirit of Wisdom came to me. May God grant me to speak as he would wish and conceive thoughts worthy of the gifts I have received, since he is both guide to Wisdom and director of sages; for we are in his hand, yes, ourselves and our sayings, and all intellectual and all practical knowledge. Wisdom 7:15,16.

§ 15. If a person wishes to study proper ethics or moral philosophy, he will find in this wisdom the surest way and the easiest Adminicula (aids). If in this life wealth is a desirable possession, what is more wealthy than Wisdom whose work is everywhere? Or if it be the intellect that is at work, who, more than she, designs whatever exists? Or if it be uprightness you love, why, virtues are the fruit of her labours, since it is she who teaches temperance and prudence, justice and fortitude; nothing in life is more useful for human beings. Or if you are eager for wide experience, she knows the past, she forecasts the future; she knows how to turn maxims and solve riddles; she has foreknowledge of signs and wonders, and of the unfolding of the ages and the times. I therefore determined to take her to share my life, knowing that she would be my counsellor in prosperity and comfort me in cares and sorrow. Wisdom 8:5-9.

§ 16. If someone wishes to study proper physics in the book of nature, he can again find no better guidance than through this divine wisdom which unites all lovers of this with the lord of nature and makes them skilled and capable so that many secrets in the creatures are revealed to them through it. As one of its students attests when he says: He it was who gave me sure knowledge of what exists, to understand the structure of the world and the action of the elements, the beginning, end and middle of the times, the alternation of the solstices and the succession of the seasons, the cycles of the year and the position of the stars, the natures of animals and the instincts of wild beasts, the powers of spirits and human mental processes, the varieties of plants and the medical properties of roots. And now I understand everything, hidden or visible, for Wisdom, the designer of all things, has instructed me. Wisdom 7:17-21.

§ 23. The most powerful means to achieve such wisdom is prayer, as James says: If any of you lacks wisdom, you should ask God, who gives generously to all without finding fault, and it will be given to you. James 1:5. Therefore, one should call on God for it from the depths of the heart saying: Grant me Wisdom, consort of your throne, and do not reject me from the number of your children. Despatch her from the holy heavens, send her forth from your throne of glory to help me and to toil with me and teach me what is pleasing to you; since she knows and understands everything, she will guide me prudently in my actions and will protect me with her glory. And who could ever have known your will, had you not given Wisdom and sent your holy Spirit from above? Thus have the paths of those on earth been straightened and people have been taught what pleases you, and have been saved, by Wisdom. Wisdom 9:4.10,11.17,18.

§ 24. However, even if a student of theology has achieved good progress in this wisdom and, through it, his heart is well-disposed so that with its help he can now provide the world a salutary service, he should not think that because of this he will gain the respect of scholars or of the noble people of the world. Because these people with their false wisdom do not recognise God in his wisdom, rather all of it appears foolish to them. 1 Corinthians 1:21. They want to know of no such wisdom which is common to all who are not scholars, and which requires in their students only godliness and justice. Therefore, they have always acted as enemies of such wisdom and, even today, they tend to persecute all its admirers and owners and call them fools and clowns.

§ 25. Keeping this in mind a lover of true wisdom must take note of what Paul says, 1 Corinthians 3:18,19, when he speaks: Do not deceive yourselves. If any of you think you are wise by the standards of this age, you should become "fools" so that you may become wise. For the wisdom of this world is foolishness in God's sight. However, even if he is despised and hated by the world, he should surely believe that God and all truly wise people in the world love him and are very pleased with him. Therefore, he should not let any adversity stop him from the study of true wisdom, but always continue with it, remembering how worthy it is to be troubled a little for such a great possession, in order that one can later receive and wear the crown of glory with honour.

THE THIRD CHAPTER

HOW IN THE STUDY OF THEOLOGY ONE SHOULD ALWAYS ACT ON, READ AND REFLECT ON GOD'S WORD

§ 1. The gracious, merciful and compassionate God could show no higher benevolence to the fallen children of men after the lamentable Fall than by again revealing his holy word to them and showing them in it clearly and in detail his divine will and advice along with the means of salvation. This divine revelation, however, did not happen suddenly and at a particular time, but gradually little by little. First God spoke through all kinds of epiphanies with our ancestors, later he had his will written by Moses and the holy prophets and, finally, he spoke to us through his Son and had the path to salvation written down perfectly by the holy evangelists and apostles. Hebrews 1:1,2.

§ 2. This revelation of the divine word did not happen only for the benefit of scholars that they alone should deal with it and form the doctrines from it. Rather, it happened for all people so that everyone who wishes to attain salvation is bound to read, to reflect and to understand this revealed word of God. However, since teachers and preachers have to understand and know it not only insofar as it is necessary for their own salvation, but also in such a deep way that from it they can show others the path and the means to salvation and present it in a thorough manner, it is necessary that they above all people should apply themselves seriously to reading and reflecting on the divine word.

§ 3. This divine word of God is the only foundation and principle of theology in its entirety. All doctrines and articles of faith must be derived from it and proven with proper arguments. Therefore, it is not enough if a theologian only reads this and that theological dogma and learns the articles of faith from them. Rather, he should draw the water of life from the correct fountain and learn to recognise God's economy in the salvation of men from the Holy Scriptures if he wishes to attain a divine conviction of the heavenly truths for himself and be able to teach them to others later with proper divine authority.

§ 4. The reading and reflection on the Holy Scriptures should not, however, be postponed till he becomes a student, but he should begin with it early on in his youth as is seen in the example of the young Timothy, of whom the holy Paul says that he was raised in faith and good teaching, which he always followed. 1 Timothy 4:6. Therefore, he also tells him, 2 Timothy 3:15, and how from infancy you have known the Holy Scriptures, which are able to make you wise for salvation through faith in Christ Jesus. And this was also the reason why the holy Paul appointed this Timothy, while he was still young, as a public teacher. And he could do great things in the Christian Church because he used the time which others spent on learning the wrongly renowned arts in the constant reading and reflection of the divine word and could thus quickly reach the purely prophetic and apostolic theology.

§ 5. Here, both parents and preceptors should heed their responsibility to diligently guide their young children, while they are in their tender years, to the Holy Scriptures and give them all kinds of good directions so that they can learn the Holy Scriptures in a useful and productive way. Certainly, except for Luther's Small Catechism, wise and true preceptors will not let the children memorise anything other than the essential sayings of the Holy Scriptures and even this in such a way that they will first explain each saying in the manner of catechism before these are committed to memory. Afterwards, they will always carry out a repetition with the sayings that have been memorised, so that what they had catechised only briefly in the beginning can now be explained through some more questions. In this way the children memorise with understanding, which sharpens their reasoning faculty, improves their will and increases their desire to learn.

§ 9. In order to benefit properly from the reading and reflection of the divine word one should not only begin with a heartfelt prayer, fervently imagining the presence of God, but one must also bring to it a hungry and thirsty heart, which is eager to understand the divine truths in the light of the Holy Spirit and also to practise them with its power and help. They will then increasingly become a part of one's life so that one can partake of all of God's promises assured to the pious in them and avoid all the bad with which the godless are threatened.

§ 10. A theologian would be acting very foolishly and unwisely if he wanted to always deal with God's word, observe the wonderful treasures of mercy in it and also recommend it highly to others while, at the same time, neither trying to look for it for himself nor really attempting to attain it and instead being satisfied with the empty letters and superficial knowledge. And this was why Christ rebuked the Jews when he says: You study the Scriptures diligently because you think that in them you have eternal life. These are the very Scriptures that testify about me, yet you refuse to come to me to have life. John 5:39,40. Similarly, there are many today who search in the Holy Scriptures, but because they do not allow a thorough change of heart to happen through penance and faith they do not want to come to Christ. Their search is thus worthy of rebuke not of praise. It leads only to adversity and finally grows into impenitence so that one becomes atheistic and has little faith in the word of God. This is because one has not devoted oneself from youth while reading, listening to and reflecting on the divine word to achieving a lived experience of all that is contained in it.

§ 16. If, therefore, a student of theology has reached this point the divine word of God will finally become a bright light which will enlighten him and bring a brilliance into his heart. With this and through him others can be enlightened about the light of the knowledge of God's glory displayed in the face of Jesus Christ. 2 Corinthians 4:6. Then he will be able to say with David: Your word is a lamp for my feet, a light on my path. Psalm 119:105. Therefore, the holy apostle Peter says: We also have the prophetic message as something completely reliable, and you will do well to pay attention to it, as to a light shining in a dark place, until the day dawns and the morning star rises in your hearts. 2 Peter 1:19.

§ 17. This word of God will refresh his soul, gladden his heart, make his mind wise and enlighten the eyes of his reason. The law of the LORD is perfect, refreshing the soul. The statutes of the LORD are trustworthy, making wise the simple. The precepts of the LORD are right, giving joy to the heart. The commands of the LORD are radiant, giving light to the eyes. Psalm 19:7,8. Indeed, it will become a proper fount of wisdom. Sirach 1:5. Because he fills all things with His wisdom, as Phison and Tigris in the time of the new fruits. He makes the understanding to abound like Euphrates, and as Jordan in the time of the harvest. He makes the doctrine of knowledge appear as the light, and as Geon in the time of vintage. Sirach 24:25-27.[3] Let therefore your mind be upon the ordinances of the Lord and meditate continually in His commandments; He will establish your heart and give you wisdom at your own desire. Sirach 6:37.

§ 20. A student of theology must therefore undertake the reading and reflection of the divine word properly and usefully so that through this not only is he led increasingly to true piety, but also to achieving such theological proficiency that he can explain it to others and present it in an edifying manner. In this, his untiring industriousness and constant prayer will help him. Also, at the same time, he will be able to avoid extensive digressions and easily attain his final goal if he can enjoy the guidance of a wise, true and experienced preceptor. Because, one tends to digress in all kinds of commentaries and is then gradually led away from the reflection on the divine word itself, through which a lot of time is wasted and much of the usefulness is lost.

§ 21. In the beginning, before one has achieved enough knowledge of the original languages, one should read the Holy Scriptures mainly for one's own edification. However, this should be done in such a way that one underlines the core sayings, repeats them often and, each time, takes one of them to meditate upon. The difficult parts, however, one should pass over till one is more experienced. If he continues like this for some time with heartfelt prayers and accustoms himself to the language of the Holy Spirit, and if he also looks for opportunities to talk about the truths learnt with his fellow-men in order to improve himself, then a

---

[3] Cf. URL: https://quranicwarners.org/sirach (last access: 18 March 2019). This passage from Sirach is taken from this site.

solid foundation for theology will have been established in him which can be built upon later properly.

§ 22. If, however, someone has not yet already achieved enough knowledge of the original languages he will continue in this and then be able to undertake the reading of the Holy Scriptures in a more accurate way. He must, especially, familiarise himself with the stories and the Sedes Materiarum (location of things, i.e. of the main passages for the biblical statements of faith) according to their order in the entire Holy Scriptures. With this the way can be paved for a hermeneutical study. However, it is necessary here to properly know the men of God who wrote the Holy Scriptures and through whom God has wrought many miracles in the world. It is necessary to know their circumstances, who and where they were, how they were appointed by God, how they behaved towards God and men, what they encountered for the sake of the truth and how God manifested himself to them. This will throw a great light on the entire Holy Scriptures.

§ 23. As far as the Sedes Materiarum are concerned, it would be useful while reading the Holy Scriptures to keep a small book at hand in which one annotates them and commits them to memory. Then he will not be hindered by the distribution of chapters but will bring everything together properly with what came earlier and what follows. He will find this easy to do in the Libris Historicis (the historical books) of both the New and the Old Testament, but the Libri Dogmatici (books of dogma) require a greater experience. However, he must also go through these and familiarise himself with them as much as he can. Especially, since the benefit will be ten times greater if he goes through the Bible systematically in this way and diligently notes down such Sedes Materiarum than if he were to use external resources extensively, which would not be useful for his memory.

§ 24. If a person has in this way gained knowledge of the main content of the Old and the New Testament so that he knows the difference between the two, and if he has also familiarised himself with the content of each of the historical books, then it is time for him to study the Holy Scriptures in their original languages. If, however, he has been hindered in learning these languages in schools, he should not allow himself to be hindered in the study of the Bible already embarked upon. Rather, he should take an accurate version with which he can move on to exegesis and practise it diligently.

§ 25. This study of exegesis requires of the diligent reader of the Holy Scriptures that he should pay careful attention to the final purpose of each book in general and of every specific matter. He should also consider all preceding, herein contained and subsequent words of every text and compare them properly with the parallel passages. But he will not be able to do this properly if he is not thoroughly acquainted with the Analogie fidei (correspondence to faith). He must also be well-versed in the Sedes Materiarum and be able to recall them from memory. It is also necessary that he properly observe the natural order and all the circumstances of each matter. In this way he will find a correct understanding of the divine word with the help of the Holy Spirit and will be able to explain it clearly.

§ 26. If a student of theology has diligently practised this, he will then have to read and reflect on the Holy Scriptures dogmatically. Thus, he must learn to understand in a beneficial manner the pure and salutary doctrine of the holy prophets and apostles in its entire concept, so that he can also explain it to his fellow-men in an edifying form. For this it becomes necessary, on the one hand, to understand God properly in his being, qualities, will, works and benefactions but he must, on the other hand, also understand man, namely how he was in his innocence, what happened to him through the lamentable Fall, how he can be saved again and brought to a condition of grace. Also, what his duties and responsibilities are, and in what kind of a prior condition he would be after his death. In order to familiarise oneself properly with all this in its proper order in the Holy Scriptures it would be useful if a person while reading and reflecting were to make small tables and thus, from God's word itself, outline the whole theology of it. Later, in all his teaching he should be guided by this, which would be of great benefit to him.

§ 27. Finally, a student of theology must also read and reflect on the Holy Scriptures in such a way that he knows how to draw correct conclusions from each verse, indeed from each word through a series of fine Porismata (sayings and sentences). In this he should have experienced how the divine truths harmonise with each other not only in the Holy Scriptures, but also in the mind, and how one always follows from the other. If he becomes familiar with the word of God, then one little word will give him an opportunity for finding many hundred edifying sayings. But he should know that neither in this nor in what has been said before will he make the desired progress if he only chooses to meditate instead of practising with other pious students, so that he can be recognised as a teacher.

THE FOURTH CHAPTER

WHY IT IS HIGHLY NECESSARY IN THE STUDY OF THEOLOGY TO BE TAUGHT BY GOD

§ 1. Having separated themselves from God through the deplorable fall from grace the children of men lost all their wisdom, sanctity and righteousness. They cannot be helped unless they submit again to God so that he rules over them again and can not only begin but also continue the work of conversion and the renewal of the lost image to bring them to salvation. For it is God who works in you to will and to act in order to fulfill his good purpose. Philippians 2:13.

§ 2. For his part, God is willing and ready to do this and obliges each person with his mercy. He is a Being who is constantly at work in all his creatures, especially with and in men as Christ says: My Father is always at his work to this very day, and I too am working. John 5:17, which the wise Sirach explains thus: but the Lord's compassion extends to everyone; rebuking, correcting and teaching, bringing them back as a shepherd brings his flock.[4] Sirach 18:13. But he always finds tremendous resistance on the part of

---

[4] URL: https://www.catholic.org/bible/book.php?id=27&bible (last access: 18 March 2019).

men, which is why he can achieve his end result only with very few in the world, as he testifies himself, when in Psalm 81:10-13 he says: I am the LORD your God, who brought you up out of Egypt. Open wide your mouth and I will fill it. But my people would not listen to me; Israel would not submit to me. So I gave them over to their stubborn hearts to follow their own devices.

§ 3. If, therefore, a person does not wish to lose God's grace that is following him and wants to be saved through it from his corruption to regain the joy of lost bliss, he must submit himself completely to God's will and open himself up to him to such an extent that he can live, work, rebuke, teach and comfort him and thus reveal his will. In this way his inner life will reflect what the Holy Scriptures say about summons, enlightenment, vindication, sanctification and all other actions of God's grace.

§ 4. If, however, all this is necessary for all men to achieve true bliss, how much more necessary it must be for a theologian who must not only achieve his own salvation with fear and trembling but must also show others the correct path to salvation and reveal all of God's advice for this. Therefore, it is not enough for such a person to be taught only by and through men, but he should also have truly let himself be taught by God if he wants to be able to say that he is God's instrument who can say with the apostle Paul: I want you to know, brothers and sisters, that the gospel I preached is not of human origin. I did not receive it from any man, nor was I taught it; rather, I received it by revelation from Jesus Christ. Galatians 1:11,12.

§ 10. Men can provide a good initiation so that a person can, with the help of the light of reason, understand both natural and spiritual truths literally and, after learning the art, also speak to others about it. But, if a person wants to reach a lived feeling for these truths and speak properly about God's wonders for the edification of his fellow-men, then God himself must teach him and give him a learned tongue. The holy David understood this when he asks God: Cause me to understand the way of your precepts, that I may meditate on your wonderful deeds. Psalm 119:27. And in the Prophet Isaiah in Chapter 50:4,5 it says: The Sovereign LORD has given me a well-instructed tongue, to know the word that sustains the weary. He wakens me morning by morning, wakens my ear to listen like one being instructed. The Sovereign LORD has opened my ears; I have not been rebellious, I have not turned away.

§ 11. The two disciples who were on their way to Emmaus could not properly understand the secrets of the Holy Scriptures despite the fact that they talked about it on the way, till Christ himself came to them and explained Moses and the prophets and the entire Holy Scriptures to them so that later they had to say: Were not our hearts burning within us while he talked with us on the road and opened the Scriptures to us? Luke 24:13-33. Thus, even if one deals with God's word thoroughly among one another no one will be able to understand the mysteries in it properly in a way that the heart is kindled by it and burns unless God himself opens his understanding and teaches him. Therefore, he should pray with David: I am your servant; give me discernment that I may understand your statutes. Psalm 119:125.

§ 12. Thus, one who wants to have blessed progress in his study of theology and, in days to come, intends to become a true servant of God in the Christian Church, he should, from his youth allow himself to be taught and instructed not only by men but also by God himself, so that he can again say with David: Since my youth, God, you have taught me, and to this day I declare your marvelous deeds. Psalm 71:17. In order to achieve this it is necessary to begin his studies with God and while hearing, reading and contemplating the Holy Scriptures to plead with God that he may receive understanding, light and wisdom. He should also lead a holy life and pay attention to the workings of God in his soul and retreat often into the silence and peace of his heart in which God through his holy word can work on him and teach him in a secret way.

§ 18. In this, namely that we should let ourselves be taught by God, our dear Saviour himself has given us an example. Because, even though he was the essential Son of God, he wanted neither to do anything by himself, nor speak or teach anything unless he had first heard and received it from his father, as he himself says: John 8:26. I have much to say in judgment of you. But he who sent me is trustworthy, and what I have heard from him I tell the world. Therefore, because even his disciples had come far, he could say to them: Matthew 10:19,20. But when they arrest you, do not worry about what to say or how to say it. At that time you will be given what to say, for it will not be you speaking, but the Spirit of your Father speaking through you.

§ 19. If then a theologian has reached a point where he always lets God himself teach him in all things, he will be such a blessed instrument that God will be able to use his church to propagate his honour and spread his truth for the salvation and well-being of many souls. In this world he will be a proper counselor and friend of God and will be comforted in his ministry by what God said to Moses: Exodus 4:15. I will help both of you speak and will teach you what to do. Indeed, God and Christ will be joined with his spirit to such an extent that with the holy Paul he can say: I will not venture to speak of anything except what Christ has accomplished through me. Romans 15:18.

THE FIFTH CHAPTER

HOW IT IS NECESSARY IN THE STUDY OF THEOLOGY TO APPLY ONESELF TO A LIVED UNDERSTANDING AND REAL EXPERIENCE OF ALL THINGS THAT ONE MUST TEACH OTHERS LATER

§ 1. A student of theology must prepare himself early for his future ministry and must diligently endeavour to ensure that he may never lack edifying matter nor the understanding to talk about it in a useful manner. For this it is not necessary to follow the advice of worldly scholars and to waste his time collecting all kinds of miscellanies (exemplary stories). Instead, through a lived understanding and practise of the divine truths he should gather a rich treasure in his heart, and he will then become, like the example of Christ, a disciple in the kingdom of heaven like the owner of a house who brings out of his storeroom new treasures as well as old. Matthew 13:52.

§ 3. The reason why many theologians, when they have to speak or write about something spiritual, are so dry and are compelled take the help of other people's books or do everything so slowly and with a vexed mind, is because they do not have a proper lived understanding nor the proper experience of such spiritual things. Rather, they are mere men of letters and thus have nothing more than letters in their brain, which require a lot of time and effort before they can be put together properly.

§ 4. Someone who travels through such a landscape himself and has seen and heard with his own eyes and ears what has transpired in it, such a person will, without much effort and on every occasion, be able to talk about it and to judge everything properly. But someone who has not travelled such a landscape himself and has only read something about it in geographical books, such a person will not only make many mistakes while narrating its condition, but will have a lot of trouble talking about it, so that he would have to consult his geography books if he wanted to talk in greater detail about it.

§ 5. Similarly, this is the difference between a person who only has a historical understanding of the divine truths and one who has a lived understanding of them. The latter is familiar with God in heaven and with the path to salvation. He has walked this path himself, and on it has experienced everything that wanderers to the invisible eternity tend to encounter, both from God as also from the Satan of the world and from their own flesh and blood. Therefore, he knows how to talk and write about it in proper detail and with very little effort, with certainty and without mistakes. But, even if the former, namely the one with only historical knowledge, finds a lot written about it in books, because he has not experienced it himself, he will not only find it difficult to retain the mere idea of it in his memory, but will also talk with fear and trembling about such unknown things. He will not know how to teach it without books and will make mistakes in everything so that his listeners will immediately know that he has neither a proper understanding nor an experience of it.

§ 6. If a person wishes to acquire a lived knowledge he should, with God's strength, begin early to practise in life what God's word prescribes. Because, if a medicus always reads many prescriptions but does not wish to prepare them himself, he would not only gain nothing from the prescriptions, but he would also not know for certain whether they were good or harmful. If, instead, he would take the species mentioned in them and prepare the prescriptions, not only would these remain firm in his memory but, after he has used them to make himself and others healthy, he would also be able to judge them properly and recommend them to others. Likewise, one who only reads the healing prescriptions for the sickness of the soul in the Holy Scriptures, but does not prepare and use them, he will not be able to judge them with certainty. One, however, who applies everything to himself, mixes it with faith and tries everything out on himself, such a person will soon arrive at a lived knowledge and will be able to judge it properly.

§ 7. Our dearest Saviour recommends this to each person as the only means of understanding the truth of his doctrine when he says: My teaching is not my own. It comes from the one who sent me. Anyone who chooses to do the will of God will find out whether my teaching comes from God or whether I speak on my own. John 7:16,17. And John declares obedience to God's commandments as the criterion of true knowledge when he says: We know that we have come to know him if we keep his commands. Whoever says, "I know him," but does not do what he commands is a liar, and the truth is not in that person. 1 John 2:3,4. One who, therefore, does in the proper order what the doctrine of Jesus prescribes about achieving divine and heavenly things, he will finally get such things himself and will thus arrive at a lived knowledge.

§ 10. A student of theology then must strive for this lived knowledge. He should not be satisfied with mere definitions of spiritual and divine things, but he should also try to ascertain whether everything is indeed as it is said, proved and believed in the Holy Scriptures and in theology. In this way he will not only gain an immutable proof and divine conviction of all theological truths, but also such solidity that later he will be able to speak, teach and write about them very clearly, seriously, powerfully and in an edifying manner without any great difficulties.

§ 11. If then a person wishes to teach others something useful and edifying about God, he should first himself be familiar with God and should have experienced since his youth God's wisdom, holiness, justice, truth, mercy, goodness, love and all other qualities. He should be practised in doing his will and should have dealt with him intimately in order to know his heart and his thoughts about his own people as well as about those who are evil. In short, he should have experienced, tasted, felt and perceived God in himself as he has revealed himself in his holy word in his Being, will and qualities. Then only will he be able to speak and teach about God in an edifying manner so that those who hear him can easily feel him in themselves and perceive that this person must be in true communion, in an ardent union and close friendship with God.

§ 14. Again, if someone wants to talk to others in detail and truthfully about conversion it is not enough to have read in books about the process which a sinner must go through for conversion. Rather, it is necessary for him to have gone through the experience himself to see what it is all about and how a soul must be prepared through penance, repentance, divine sorrow, all kinds of spiritual struggles, strife and challenges in order to face God's strict judgment, and he must experience the fear of hell. Afterwards, however, through faith in the mercy of Jesus Christ he will be absolved, washed in his holy blood and, through his strength, be completely changed and renewed in his heart, his mind, his soul, his reason and will. If all this has taken place in him it will be very easy for him to teach it not only clearly and thoroughly, but also powerfully and in an edifying manner.

§ 15. If a person wants to talk to others about the condition of grace in a salutary manner and present everything that happens in it in a systematic and edifying form to every child of God it is again necessary that he have a lived and real experience of the rebirth, of the justification, of the enlightenment, of sanctification, of the filiation and union of God, of the effects of the Holy Spirit and of all other acts of mercy. Only then will he have allowed himself in deed and truth to be reborn, justified, enlightened, sanctified and brought through filiation to a union with God, and he would be driven by the Holy Spirit. After that he will be able to talk freely and with great usefulness about the condition of grace and everyone will be astonished.

§ 16. If a person wants to present something useful about the cross borne by Christians and about their spiritual enemies as well as about the struggle against these in order to comfort and enlighten others, then this can similarly only happen if he first allows himself to try it and be tested in it. Thus, for the sake of true piety, he will experience the hate, disfavour, scorn, mockery, disdain and persecution of the world and will get to know the devil in his tricks, the world in its temptation, his flesh and blood in its cajoling. With God's strength he will struggle and fight against it and learn how to win. Through patient composure in the face of many spiritual temptations he will arrive at a knowledge of the wonderful ways of God. Afterwards he will be able to teach it so fruitfully and powerfully that one would have to admit that he has experienced all this himself.

§ 17. If, therefore, a student of theology was to follow this advice and practise it in schools as well as in universities he would, when in his ministry, be very proficient at teaching and preaching about all theological matters from his own experience without any difficulty. Indeed, I can assure him that if he carries out his study of theology in this manner and adopts the meaning, spirit, life and behaviour of the holy apostles and men of God he will gradually achieve their proficiency and will be able to talk, teach and preach freely without books and notes about all spiritual matters at every opportunity with great benefit for others.

The Sixth Chapter

How a person should be tested and tried in the study of theology through all kinds of suffering and temptations

§ 1. In schools and in the church, children always hear a lot about Christianity from their teachers: what it is, what it is made up of, how it should be practised and what is the grace of God to be expected from it. But they cannot become upright Christians until they experience tribulations so that the good teachings that have till now only been in their minds can gain proper strength in them and can be reflected upon and tried out. Therefore, one sees that those people are the best Christians who have been tested and tried the most, whereas those who know little of suffering and temptations carry their Christianity only in their mouths and brains.

§ 2. Similarly, when in schools and universities students of theology only hear, read and debate about holy theology without having experienced its power and effect through all kinds of trials, they cannot be upright theologians and cannot serve or be useful to God in a public ministry. If, however, they have been properly tested and made pliant in their study of theology through tribulations and suffering then they can not only unlock the seal of the Holy Scriptures that are full of tribulation, but they are also in a position for God to use them in all events for the conversion of men.

§ 5. The holy Prophet Isaiah says in Chapter 28:19 that only suffering teaches one to heed the word. If theologians, therefore, have no tribulations, they will, it is sure, always deal with God's word, will hear it, read and reflect on it but will not think that it has also been written and said for them. They will also not see in it the mystery of the cross which is described on all pages, but they will only concern themselves with all kinds of Adminicula (aids), with the help of which they can explain it to others and thus carry out their business with them. O, how wretched it is when such people later must talk about God's word and explain the mystery of the cross to others.

§ 6. Such theologians who have little experience of suffering and temptations and who have grown up with good days and a pleasant life—they will neither understand nor believe the doctrine of Jesus Christ properly. Especially since the entire theology of our Saviour is nothing other than the message of the cross. 1 Corinthians 1:18. And, if they had not been born into Christianity and had not been taught this doctrine from their youth, which they then accepted on the authority of their parents and teachers, they would debate much more passionately against this doctrine of the cross than they now tend to do against the foolishness of idolatry. Because, as long as a person is still living in his unbroken nature the mystery of the cross will remain for him a foolishness, even if he were very learned and could teach and preach much about the cross.

§ 7. If a person enters a public ministry and has not been tested beforehand under the cross, he will not have the ability to deal with weary, troubled souls in spiritual sorrow. The comforting sentences he utters to such distressed souls will come from books and not from his own experience and will not move or calm the heart. His talks will pull them down rather than build them up. If he too is then confronted with all kinds of unpleasantness in his work, he will become impatient and will prefer to neglect the good rather than putting up with any trouble or hardship for its sake. He does not aspire to practising an honest Christianity so that he is not persecuted for the cross of Christ. Galatians 6:12.

§ 9. Those, therefore, who are honest theologians say with the holy Paul: we also glory in our sufferings, because we know that suffering produces perseverance; perseverance, character; Romans 5:3,4. Because, suffering and the beloved cross drives such theologians to prayer so that they may acquaint themselves better with the crucified Christ. It leads them to read the Scriptures diligently and it sharpens their reason to such an extent that they can properly see how God always dealt with his people. Thus, the mystery of the cross will be unlocked for them and they can now read the Holy Scriptures with completely new eyes and with a completely new tongue they can explain it according to the Holy Spirit. Through this they will also learn to understand worldly vanities so that they can deny these and only aspire for invisible and eternal things. And, in this way, through suffering and tribulations they will receive an experience that is worth its weight in gold. Because, a man practised in this understands a lot and a well-experienced man can speak of wisdom. One, however, who is not practised in this understands little. Sirach 34:9,10.

§ 15. However, even though suffering is highly necessary for a theologian, he should not bear a cross of his own making, nor struggle imprudently for this or that misfortune. Because, everything that he brings upon himself through his sins is not a proper cross but a just punishment. If he only denies the world and guides his students in schools and universities to lead a devout and pious life and to learn to punish the world in its evil, and if he teaches them to practise the will of God he will soon be despised, hated, mocked and persecuted by the world. If he then remains constant in his intentions and strives diligently to struggle and battle against the evil desires of his flesh, against the seduction of the world and against the cunning temptation of the devil, he will have enough of a cross. If he, in addition, wishes to put all his theology into practice and give himself up completely to God, he will then be introduced to real spiritual temptations and will be tested by God himself in many ways. However, he will not be tempted beyond what he can endure. 1 Corinthians 10:13.

PASSAGES FROM THE OTHER SEVEN PARTS
IN WHICH ZIEGENBALG TOUCHES UPON
THE SITUATION IN TRANQUEBAR

THE FIFTH PART, THE THIRD CHAPTER

MAKING USE OF
SPECIAL OPPORTUNITIES TO PREACH

§ 13. One could object and say that this kind of thing happened when the Christian Church had to be established, and it is not necessary now since this has been accomplished. Therefore, one should be satisfied with the usual teaching in the church. However, a person who properly examines and judges present-day Christianity not according to the stone churches built and to the number of theological books found in them, but according to the life and conduct of the Christians, will find that this kind of teaching, besides the public sermons, is just as necessary today as it was then, and that the former do not bear much fruit without the latter. Because, even if a preacher preaches wonderful teachings from the pulpit, but, later, when he mingles with the people, only talks of worldly things, the people will think that it will not be wrong to leave such teachings behind in the church since the teacher himself does not carry his teachings beyond the pulpit.

§ 14. I have especially found among the heathens here that this way of teaching has been ten times more useful than when I preached publicly from the pulpit in their language. Because, even though many heathens came to our Jerusalem church when we preached or catechized in it, I always had far greater access to such heathens if I was in the countryside or in a place convenient to them, where a large crowd always gathered and often listened to me for many hours. In this way, a vast knowledge of Christianity could be spread far and wide among the heathens here. Therefore, their anger is even greater, since they hear everywhere that I have been imprisoned by my co-believers for this. However, the gospel is not restrained, rather it leads Christians and heathens to even greater contemplation when they ponder over the signs of these times and remember all that they heard from me, so that I can say with Paul: Now I want you to know, brothers and sisters, that what has happened to me has actually served to advance the gospel. As a result, it has become clear throughout the whole palace guard and to everyone else that I am in chains for Christ. And because of my chains, most of the brothers and sisters have become confident in the Lord and dare all the more to proclaim the gospel without fear. Philippians 1:12-14.

PREACHING CAN ALSO BE DONE IN A WRITTEN FORM, EVEN FROM PRISON

§ 18. God, for his holy reasons, allowed his faithful servant Jeremiah to be put in prison by the evil of those he was trying to save out of heartfelt love and for the testimony of truth. But he still showed Jeremiah an opportunity to be of greater use in prison through his writing than if he had been free. Similarly, God in his wise counsel has allowed that I, his unworthy servant, am placed in this prison of mine for the sake of the truth. However, even though I do not have the liberty here that Jeremiah had to use ink and quill, God in his wondrous way has ordained that I can write this book for the benefit of my fellow-brothers without the knowledge of my enemies. Even if it should initially be hated by some because I could not write anything other than the truth, I hope that like the writings of the imprisoned Jeremiah and the restrained Paul it will later be of some use to many people, even if it is after my death, especially since the writings of the holy men of God were canonised only after their death. While they were alive, they had to be heretics, seducers and agitators since their earnest life was unbearable to others.

The Fifth Part, the Tenth Chapter

Self-examination before Holy Communion

§10. This examination requires so much time that it is difficult to carry it out properly only in the confessional. This is especially true where there are large congregations so that one often has no time for absolution, much less to carry out a proper examination with each person individually. Therefore, teachers and preachers must arrange that all penitents report to them at least eight days in advance and during this time examine themselves and the condition of their hearts. This arrangement is prevalent here in our small congregation from the heathens so that no one may come to the confessional if he has not allowed himself to be examined and taught for eight days prior to that.

Practice of Child-Baptism

§ 16. One should baptise either only small children or adults from the heathens, Jews and Turks. As far as the baptism of children is concerned, one should assume that they have faith although they still cannot think for themselves. Thus, their faith can neither be examined nor can they be converted before baptism. However, it is the duty and the obligation of a teacher to give good lessons about baptism to those children he has baptised and who are now able to understand it, and to show them thoroughly and clearly what

God promised them and what they promised God in baptism. He should also show that God cannot keep up his union with them unless they observe their promises and submit to his order. If teachers do not do this and, instead, let the baptised children remain without this teaching and frequent repetition of their baptismal union they will be held strictly accountable for this.

PRACTICE OF ADULT-BAPTISM

§ 17. As far as the baptism of adults is concerned, it should, as decreed by Christ, be preceded by instruction so that they give an account of their faith in such a way that one also sees certain qualities of true penitence in them. That is why we read in Matthew 3:8.10,11 that those who let themselves be baptised by John confessed their sins, whereupon he exhorted them sharply to repent, saying: Produce fruit in keeping with repentance. The ax is already at the root of the trees, and every tree that does not produce good fruit will be cut down and thrown into the fire. I baptize you with water for repentance. Afterwards we see from the holy apostles that they never baptised a person unless they had first instructed him in the faith of Jesus and heard his confession.

§ 18. We follow all this as far as possible here among the heathens. Especially since no heathen is baptised before he has memorized Luther's Small Catechism in his language, and this is done in such a way that it is explained to him word by word very simply and clearly and always applied to his life. After that, and before baptism, he is examined publicly about all the articles of faith so that he must reply to each question in his own words. After receiving baptism, he still gets individual instruction daily for a few months before he can partake of Holy Communion.

THE FIFTH PART, THE ELEVENTH CHAPTER

CATECHISM IS HERE OFTEN MORE EFFECTIVE THAN A SERMON

§ 7. With God's grace we have instituted such arrangements here among the heathens in our Jerusalem-congregation that every day there is private catechism four times in our houses, twice in Portuguese and twice in the Malabarian language, while publicly catechism is conducted twice a week in the church. Every time more heathens come to listen to this than to a sermon. The former is far more useful for our congregation than the latter, especially since they are all new beginners in Christianity and still must eat infant-food. This has, however, now been denied to them in their mother-tongue for a long time because I have had to sit in prison till date.

MEETINGS IN THE HOUSE HAVE A BIBLICAL EXAMPLE

§ 11. Accordingly, an orthodox teacher is not at fault if, along with public teaching, he also instructs his listeners privately in God's word and, to this end, holds a Christian assembly in his house. He can do this if everything is done properly and is geared towards edification. Because, if a person can hold a Bible course or a theological lecture for students in his house, then a teacher may be allowed to deal with God's word for his listeners in his house, especially since the latter are bound more closely with his conscience than students of theology are with the conscience of their professor. And, if a pure theologian has control over such meetings then one need not be afraid of confusion or other negative things.

HOUSE-MEETINGS EVEN IN TRANQUEBAR

§ 13. Thus, even if a teacher will be persecuted for it, he should not abstain from such edifying arrangements in the certain assurance that they will, with God's blessings, be very beneficial. I have experienced this myself here in this heathen country, especially since many European Christians requested us to explain the Holy Scriptures to them privately in our mother-tongue. We saw this as a welcome opportunity for edification and granted their wish at once, so that we took out an hour every day for this and I have explained the four evangelists to them word for word. In the Acts we have reached the 16th Chapter till the imprisonment of the holy Paul. At that point I was put in prison despite my innocence, which is why we have had to stop there, while my colleague continues it mornings and evenings with his own people. The edification that is achieved in this manner can be seen in those who heard it and afterwards reflected on it on the seas in the face of many dangers. Thereupon, they did not know how they should show their gratitude to us.

THE FIFTH PART, THE TWELFTH CHAPTER

HELP THE YOUNG CONGREGATION IN TRANQUEBAR!

§ 15. Every teacher in his concern for the poor should faithfully follow this example of the holy apostle Paul if he wishes to fulfil the duty of his conscience and of his ministry adequately. God in his grace found me worthy of propagating the gospel here among the heathens and, thereby, propagating the Christian religion. But I see with great distress that our newly-planted congregation of Jerusalem faces great poverty and is deprived of all human help.

Thus, my heartfelt prayers and entreaties go out to all evangelical teachers and preachers who might get to read this book that they share the heartfelt grief for them with me and endeavour to see how the kingdom of Jesus Christ here among the heathens can be set up and spread through the charity of benevolent Christians in Europe. And, even though I must stay in prison now for this, I am sure through these afflictions the foundation of our Jerusalem will be so deep that the gates of hell will not be able to vanquish the congregation of Christ placed in it.

The Sixth Part, the Third Chapter

Why I read heathen books

§ 4. With this I do not wish to say that a Christian theologian cannot read heathen books and examine in what blindness such people have lived, how far they have been able to come in their knowledge of natural things and what they believe about God and life hereafter. I too live here in such conditions among the heathens that for the sake of my work I have had to read their books almost daily, partly in order to learn their language thoroughly, but partly also to familiarise myself with all the principles of their heathenism from their own doctrines in order to be able to show them orally and in writing the truth of our Christian religion and the falsity of their heathen idolatry. I then find many philosophical disciplines in their books, but I did not read them in order to teach them or to debate about theology with them in this form. Rather, I wanted to be able to show them from all this how their alleged wisdom in divine and natural matters is only foolishness, and how it hinders them from true conversion and from achieving proper wisdom.

THE SEVENTH PART, THE FIRST CHAPTER

PERSECUTION IN TRANQUEBAR

§ 9. Here among the heathens my dear colleague and I have suffered a somewhat similar fate and have had to endure from the Christians what Paul at that time had to endure from his people, the Jews. Because, as far as the heathens and Mohammedans are concerned, they always like to listen to us and associate with us and consider it a great pleasure to discuss religious matters with us. Therefore, every time I visited their schools or went into the countryside, many of them would gather around me and they not only listened to the propagation of the gospel, but also asked me all kinds of things about God, about the soul, about life hereafter and other edifying things. They also arrived at a conviction of the truth and applauded my words even if they could not resolve immediately to accepting Christianity. But the badly-behaved Christians, and indeed not so much the Catholics but rather the Lutherans who should have the greatest joy in such works, always opposed us strongly and finally carried their tyranny so far that they dismissed me from my ministry against heathenism and placed me in prison. The heathens far and near are in great dismay at this turn of events.

§ 10. Despite all this I am comforted in the Lord and consider this a sign that God will open a big door to the heathens for me, especially since there is great agitation among them and the words in which I spoke to them every day are only now being reflected upon properly. At all times the Christian Church has similarly had its beginning, its growth and progress amidst great affliction and severe persecution. What happened to Christ and all the holy apostles for the sake of the truth need not then bring shame to me; instead I have more reason to be very happy about it, saying with the imprisoned Paul: This is my gospel, for which I am suffering even to the point of being chained like a criminal. But God's word is not chained. Therefore I endure everything for the sake of the elect, that they too may obtain the salvation that is in Christ Jesus, with eternal glory. 2 Timothy 2:9,10.

THE SEVENTH PART, THE NINTH CHAPTER

IMPRISONED – LIKE MICAIAH

§ 2. The Prophet Micaiah had done nothing other than tell the truth according to God's command and on the request of King Ahab in the presence of four hundred false prophets. Yet, he was not only beaten up for this, but he was also imprisoned as we read in 1 Kings 22:23-28, where it says: So now the LORD has put a deceiving spirit in the mouths of all these prophets of yours. The LORD has decreed disaster for you. Then Zedekiah son of Kenaanah went up and slapped Micaiah in the face. "Which way did the spirit from the LORD go when he went from me to speak to you?" he asked. Micaiah replied, "You will find out on the day you go to hide in an inner room." The king of Israel then ordered, "Take Micaiah and send him back to Amon the ruler of the city and to Joash the king's son and say, 'This is what the king says: Put this fellow in prison and give him nothing but bread and water until I return safely.'" Micaiah declared, "If you ever return safely, the LORD has not spoken through me." Then he added, "Mark my words, all you people!" Let just one among the teachers today follow this Prophet Micaiah and, with similar delight, tell the rulers the truth, then he will, like me, suffer the same fate as Micaiah. I cannot see when my imprisonment will end, especially since I have now been compelled with even greater delight to demonstrate the truth that has been suppressed till now and against which one continues to barricade oneself.

IMPRISONED – LIKE PAUL

§ 8. This is also what happened to the holy Paul with his faithful companion Silas. When they were propagating the word of the Lord to the heathens at Philippi the people were instigated against them and the magistrate ordered that they be stripped and beaten with rods. After they had been severely flogged, they were thrown into prison, and the jailer was commanded to guard them carefully. When he received these orders, he put them in the inner cell and fastened their feet in the stocks. Acts 16:22-24. Although they were saved this time by God's miraculous hand, Paul was again taken prisoner, beaten and bound with two chains. Acts 21:32,33. He was in prison for more than four years and had to suffer a lot of humiliation at the hands of the Jews. Acts 24:27; Acts 28:30. Nevertheless, he had the opportunity to propagate the gospel of Christ both orally and in writing. Most of his epistles were written during his imprisonment, so that he almost achieved more while in prison than when he was free. This gives me a lot of comfort in the hope that my imprisonment will similarly be of benefit to the Christian Church.

THE EIGHTH PART, THE FOURTH CHAPTER

I TOO AM IMPRISONED LIKE JEREMIAH

§ 11. Finally, after the city of Jerusalem was won from the Chaldeans according to Jeremiah's prophecy, he saw with his own eyes how all his enemies had to die and were badly tormented, but he alone was saved and regarding with great mercy by the king Nebuchadnezzar as is written in Jeremiah 39:11-14. Now Nebuchadnezzar king of Babylon had given these orders about Jeremiah through Nebuzaradan commander of the imperial guard: "Take him and look after him; don't harm him but do for him whatever he asks." [Jeremiah 39:12.] So Nebuzaradan the commander of the guard, Nebushazban a chief officer, Nergal-Sharezer a high official and all the other officers of the king of Babylon sent and had Jeremiah taken out of the courtyard of the guard. They turned him over to Gedaliah, son of Ahikam, the son of Shaphan, to take him back to his home. So he remained among his own people. Thus, Jeremiah was accepted and treated far better by the heathens than by his own people, the Jews, who caused him much grief. Just as I too have experienced here that I have always been persecuted by my own co-religionists for the sake of the truth, while all the heathens, on the other hand, loved me. If their will were to prevail, I would be set free from my prison soon, even though I always spoke passionately against their idolatry. However, I hope that I will be saved by God when, according to his will, I will have given a written testimony.

THE NINTH PART, THE FIRST CHAPTER

(AS AN EXAMPLE OF ZIEGENBALG'S USE OF THE SCRIPTURES)

ABOUT THE DIFFERENT NAMES FOR TEACHERS AND PREACHERS

§ 1. Pious teachers and preachers have many names in the Holy Scriptures through which their inner qualities as well as their outward responsibilities to God and men are indicated and expressed. In order that they do not carry such lovely names in vain and always remember their obligation to it and live according to it in their holy ministry, I will list seventeen important names and give them an opportunity to not only reflect on them properly, but also to lead their life and conduct their work in such a way that in deed and truth they can see what such names mean and what they demand of them.

§ 2. Firstly, teachers and preachers are called seers in the Holy Scriptures, the name the Prophet Samuel had as we read in 1 Samuel 9:18,19 where Saul says to Samuel: Would you please tell me where the seer's house is? "I am the seer," Samuel replied. "Go up ahead of me to the high place, for today you are to eat with me, and in the morning I will send you on your way and will tell you all that is in your heart. Similarly, the Prophet Amos was called a seer when the priest Amaziah spoke to him: Get out, you seer! Go back to the land of Judah. Earn your bread there and do your prophesying there. Amos 7:12. What, however, a seer is we see in Numbers 24:3,4 where it is shown that the seer is a man whose eyes see clearly, who hears the words of God, who sees a vision from the Almighty, who falls prostrate and whose eyes are opened. If teachers and preachers today still want to be proper seers they must, through constant prayer, not only get enlightened eyes with which they can look into the mysteries of the divine word, but they should also have acquired such spiritual hearing that they can always hear the voice of God when they reflect on the Holy Scriptures and they must strive to follow it.

§ 3. Secondly, teachers and preachers are also called prophets as is said in 1 Samuel 9:9 Formerly in Israel, if someone went to inquire of God, they would say, "Come, let us go to the seer," because the prophet of today used to be called a seer. And, in the following Chapter 10:5 Samuel tells Saul: After that you will go to Gibeah of God, where there is a Philistine outpost. As you approach the town, you will meet a procession of prophets coming down from the high place with lyres, timbrels, pipes and harps being played before them, and they will be prophesying. In 1 Kings 20:35 there is remembrance of a man among the company of the prophets, and in 2 Kings 2:3 the company of the prophets who were in Bethlehem went to Elisha and said to him: Do you know that the LORD is going to take your master from you today? Similarly, in Chapter 4:38 it says Elisha returned to Gilgal and there was a famine in that region and the company of the prophets met with him. And in the following Chapter 6:1 it says: The company of the prophets said to Elisha, "Look, the place where we meet with you is too small for us. From all this one sees that in those times all teachers were called prophets and their students were called company of prophets. That is why this name is also given to teachers in the New Testament. Matthew 23:34. If they want to have the right to carry this name, they must be very familiar with the great Prophet Christ Jesus and know the will of God and all his advice. They should also have come so far in the school of the Holy Spirit that they can proclaim future blessings to the pious and future ill to the godless.

§ 4. Thirdly, teachers and preachers are called men of God because, on the one hand, they live in an ardent association with God and allow God to use them in the world and, on the other hand, also because they search, speak and do only what is divine, what comes from God and leads to God. We read about such a man of God in 1 Kings 13:1, where it says: By the word of the LORD a man of God came from Judah to Bethel and he cried out against the altar. Later, in Chapter 17:24 we read that a woman spoke thus to the Prophet Elijah: Now I know that you are a man of God and that the word of the LORD from your mouth is the truth. Also, in 2 Kings 1:9 the captain of the king Ahazia said to Elijah: Man of God, the king says, 'Come down!' Even Elisha was called a man of God since in Chapter 4:9 a woman talks about him to her husband: I know that this man who often comes our way is a holy man of God. Just as this can also be seen in the following chapters: Chapter 5:15; 6:6.9; 7:2; 8:7.

§ 5. This name has also been given to teachers and preachers in the New Testament as we see in the example of the young Timothy to whom Paul writes: But you, man of God, flee from all this, and pursue righteousness, godliness, faith, love, endurance and gentleness. 1 Timothy 6:11. In 2 Timothy 3:17 it also says that a man of God is thoroughly equipped for all good work. If, therefore, teachers and preachers today want to carry this name honourably, they should have participated in the divine nature 2 Peter 1:4. They should show through their person the divine qualities of justice, godliness, wisdom, truth, love and goodness, and look only for the divine in the world. Thus, they should be in such an ardent union with God that he can always use them according to his will to propagate his honour in the world. In this way people can also see that something divine is shining forth in their life, their words and their works.

§ 6. Fourthly, teachers and preachers are also called fathers in the Holy Scriptures as Elisha calls the Prophet Elijah when he called out to him and spoke: My father, my father! 2 Kings 2:12. And, in the following chapter 6:21 the king of Israel called the Prophet Elisha his father and said: Shall I kill them, my father? Shall I kill them? Similarly, the king Jehoash as is said in chapter 13:14: Now Elisha had been suffering from the illness from which he died. Jehoash king of Israel went down to see him and wept over him. "My father! My father!" he cried, "the chariots and horsemen of Israel!" Even in the New Testament the name father is given to teachers and the reason mentioned is because they are mediators in the spiritual rebirth of their listeners as we see in the example of Paul who writes about himself and his Corinthians in 1 Corinthians 4:14,15: I am writing this not to shame you but to warn you as my dear children. Even if you had ten thousand guardians in Christ, you do not have many fathers, for in Christ Jesus I became your father through the gospel. And in Galatians 4:19 he says: My dear children, for whom I am again in the pains of childbirth until Christ is formed in you.

§ 7. If, therefore, even today teachers and preachers wish to be called spiritual fathers then they should not remain as children in their Christianity who allow themselves to by swayed by all kinds of winds about the doctrine, but mature men attaining to the whole measure of the fullness of Christ. Ephesians 4:13,14. Because children cannot beget children until they have reached a mature age. If teachers and preachers want to produce spiritual children, it is imperative that they achieve this mature age in Christ and are complete people whose senses are accustomed to distinguishing between good and evil. Hebrews 5:14. They must themselves be reborn, justified, enlightened, sanctified and renewed by God if they are to work properly in the rebirth, justification, enlightenment, sanctification and renewal of their listeners. After that they should show them paternal love and always ensure that day by day they grow and advance in their Christianity, and that their children become young men, the young men become men and fathers.

§ 8. Fifthly, in God's holy word teachers and preachers are also called the voice of the Lord through whom the advice and will of God resounds and is trumpeted across the world. Psalm 29:3-9 talks of such a voice: The voice of the Lord is over the waters; The voice of the Lord is powerful; the voice of the Lord is majestic. He makes Lebanon leap like a calf. The voice of the Lord strikes with flashes of lightning. The voice of the Lord shakes the Desert of Kadesh. The voice of the Lord twists the oaks and strips the forests bare. And in his temple all cry, "Glory!" In Isaiah 40:3 it says: A voice of one calling: In the wilderness prepare the way for the Lord; make straight the way for our God. In Matthew 3:3 this is understood to be a reference to John the Baptist. Therefore, when he was asked by the Jews through a delegation who he was, he replied in the words of Isaiah the Prophet: I am the voice of one calling in the wilderness. 'Make straight the way for the Lord.' John 1:23. In this way, even today every honest teacher is a voice of the Lord when he hands over his heart, his feelings, his soul, reason and will in such a way to God that God can talk through him, preach through him and be effective in him. But this requires that one is not dull, half-hearted and idle in one's ministry, but that one raises one's voice like a trumpet and calls out to reliable people: Wake up, sleeper, rise from the dead, and Christ will shine on you. Ephesians 5:14.

§ 9. In the sixth-place teachers and preachers are also called leaders because they lead people who have gone astray away from the path of damnation and show them the correct path to salvation. They also walk ahead of them on this path and thus, both with their teaching and their life, they should lead them to heaven. But usually God has had to lament about evil leaders among his people as we read in Isaiah 9:16, where it says: Those who guide this people mislead them, and those who are guided are led astray. And in Matthew 15:14 Christ says of the Pharisees: Leave them; they are blind guides. If the blind lead the blind, both will fall into a pit." Even Paul talks Romans 2:19 about people who presume to lead the blind, but who themselves do wrong. Therefore, if a teacher does not want to be a blind, but rather a wise and experienced leader of souls, he should have wandered on those paths of God to which he wants to direct others into a communion with God with the joy of eternal salvation. He must let himself be directed and led by God and always have the Holy Spirit living in him who can lead him in all truth. Then he will carry this name with honour and bring about a lot of good in his ministry.

§ 10. In the seventh instance teachers and preachers are called watchmen in the Holy Scriptures as it says Isaiah 52:8: Your watchmen lift up their voices; together they shout for joy. When the LORD returns to Zion, they will see it with their own eyes. And, in the following chapter 62:6 it says: I have posted watchmen on your walls, Jerusalem; they will never be silent day or night. You who call on the LORD, give yourselves no rest. In Jeremiah 6:17 also it says: I appointed watchmen over you and said, 'Listen to the sound of the trumpet!' And the Lord spoke to the Prophet Ezekiel: "Son of man, I have made you a watchman for the people of Israel; so hear the word I speak and give them warning from me. Ezekiel 3:17. If teachers and preachers want to be worthy of this name they must always be on their guard and be found vigilant in their ministry because they have powerful and cunning enemies around them who try just as hard to abduct the souls from God and hand them over to Satan as they are trying to pull them away from Satan's grasp and lead them to God. This vigilance of theirs should be combined with true loyalty and constancy so that they are not lulled into safety either by the rough winds of temptation or by the gentle breeze of worldly vanity.

§ 11. In the eighth instance teachers and preachers are often called angels or messengers of God in the Holy Scriptures as is said in Isaiah 52:7: How beautiful on the mountains are the feet of those who bring good news, who proclaim peace, who bring good tidings, who proclaim salvation, who say to Zion, "Your God reigns!" And Malachi 2:7 it says: For the lips of a priest ought to preserve knowledge, and people seek instruction from his mouth, because he is an angel of the Lord Zebaoth. In the following chapter 3:1 it is said: I will send my messenger, who will prepare the way before me. In the New Testament this is said to refer to John. Matthew 11:10. Similarly, the seven teachers or bishops of the seven congregations in Asia are called angels. Revelation 2:1.8.12.18; Revelation 3:1.7.14. Those teachers who want to honour this name should be true emissaries of God and should have a divine and legitimate calling to their ministry. They should also carry their message well to the people always remembering the account they will have to render to their Lord hereafter. They should live like messengers of God in this world and strive to follow the holy angels in their wisdom and holiness so that after their mission is completed, they can enter the company of angels with honour.

§ 12. In the ninth instance teachers and preachers are called shepherds as God himself says in Jeremiah 3:15: Then I will give you shepherds after my own heart, who will lead you with knowledge and understanding. And in Chapter 23:4 he says: I will place shepherds over them who will tend them, and they will no longer be afraid or terrified, nor will any be missing," declares the LORD. Christ also speaks about this when he says John 10:1-4: Very truly I tell you, anyone who does not enter the sheep pen by the gate, but climbs in by some other way, is a thief and a robber. The one who enters by the gate is the shepherd of the sheep. The gatekeeper opens the gate for him, and the sheep listen to his voice. He calls his own sheep by name and leads them out. When he has brought out all his own, he goes on ahead of them, and his sheep follow him because they know his voice. Thus, because teachers and preachers are spiritual shepherds they should have been led into the sheep-pen of the Christian Church by the Holy Spirit. They should be faithful like shepherds so that they can get to know the inner condition of the souls entrusted to them and call each one of them by their name, they should always let them frolic in the meadows of the divine word and lead them by example so that these souls can see that they are good shepherds whose voice they should hear and whose example they should follow.

§ 13. In the tenth instance teachers and preachers are also called lights as Christ declares when he speaks to his disciples Matthew 5:14-16: You are the light of the world. A town built on a hill cannot be hidden. Neither do people light a lamp and put it under a bowl. Instead they put it on its stand, and it gives light to everyone in the house. In the same way, let your light shine before others, that they may see your good deeds and glorify your Father in heaven. Jewish teachers also laid claim to such names and called themselves a light for those who are in darkness. Romans 2:19. However, if teachers and preachers today want to lay legitimate claim to this name, their souls should be truly enlightened, and the Holy Spirit should always live in their reason and their will. They should also conduct themselves as children of the light so that those who are in darkness and in the shadow of death can find the light for their conversion by looking at the devout life of these teachers and preachers and by listening to their salutary teachings. 2 Corinthians 4:6; Acts 26:18.

§ 14. In the eleventh instance the Holy Scriptures call teachers and preachers witnesses, because with their teaching and their life they should bear true witness to all divine truths. John the Baptist bore this name as is said John 1:6-8: There was a man sent from God whose name was John. He came as a witness to testify concerning that light, so that through him all might believe. He himself was not the light; he came only as a witness to the light. Therefore, in the following verse 15 it says: John testified concerning him. He cried out, saying, this is the one I spoke about when I said, He who comes after me has surpassed me because he was before me. And, in verse 32: Then John gave this testimony: I saw the Spirit come down from heaven as a dove and remain on him. I have seen and I testify that this is God's Chosen One. Verse 34. This name was also given to the holy apostles when Christ speaks to them thus in John 15:27: And you also must testify, for you have been with me from the beginning. In Acts 1:8 he tells them: But you will receive power when the Holy Spirit comes on you; and you will be my witnesses in Jerusalem, and in all Judea and Samaria, and to the ends of the earth. The apostles faithfully honoured this name as is said in Acts 4:33: With great power the apostles continued to testify to the resurrection of the Lord Jesus. And God's grace was powerfully at work in them all.

§ 15. Acts 5:32 also says about this: We are witnesses of these things, and so is the Holy Spirit, whom God has given to those who obey him. Similarly, chapter 10:39-43: We are witnesses of everything he did in the country of the Jews and in Jerusalem. They killed him by hanging him on a cross, but God raised him from the dead on the third day and caused him to be seen. He was not seen by all the people, but by witnesses whom God had already chosen—by us who ate and drank with him after he rose from the dead. He commanded us to preach to the people and to testify that he is the one whom God appointed as judge of the living and the dead. All the prophets testify about him that everyone who believes in him receives forgiveness of sins through his name. Paul was also ordained as such a witness as he himself says that Ananias told him: The God of our ancestors has chosen you to know his will and to see the Righteous One and to hear words from his mouth. You will be his witness to all people of what you have seen and heard. Acts 22:14,15; Acts 26:16 and Revelation 1:12 the evangelist John calls himself a servant of God who has borne witness to the word of God and the testimony of Jesus Christ.

§ 16. If then faithful teachers and preachers wish to follow in the footsteps of the apostles and be honest witnesses of Christ and his truth, they should have seen and heard everything as a lived experience with spiritual eyes and ears if they want to bear witness to it before the world and among people as a divine and certain truth. They should know Christ well and the Holy Spirit should live and work in them as the proper witness of truth so that he can teach them everything and always remind them of all that Christ taught and spoke. John 14:26; 15:26. They must also truly believe what they preach to others as the necessary articles of faith and thus show through their life and conduct that the testimony they bear outwardly to the world is also in their hearts. They should also be determined not only to endure all kinds of trouble, suffering, humiliation, scorn, ridicule and persecution for the sake of the truth, but also to seal this truth with their blood if it is the will of the Saviour.

§ 17. In the twelfth instance teachers and preachers are called disciples of the Lord in God's word as we see in the example of the apostles. Matthew 5:1; 8:21; 10:1; 11:1. The Saviour indicates the distinguishing feature of such disciples with these words when he says John 13:35: By this everyone will know that you are my disciples, if you love one another. On the other hand, he says in Luke 14:26,27.33: If anyone comes to me and does not hate father and mother, wife and children, brothers and sisters—yes, even their own life—such a person cannot be my disciple. And whoever does not carry their cross and follow me cannot be my disciple. In the same way, those of you who do not give up everything you have cannot be my disciples. Therefore, if today also teachers and preachers want to be honest disciples of Christ they must always sit at his holy feet and learn from him everything that his disciples must know and practise in life. They must renounce themselves, the world and everything that belongs to the world and, in patient composure under the cross, they must follow their Lord faithfully. They should also have a binding brotherly love amongst themselves so that everyone can see that they do not take an interest in the world but only in Christ and carry out their ministry according to this.

§ 18. Besides this, in the thirteenth instance, teachers and preachers are called leaders in the Holy Scriptures as it says in Hebrews 13:7. Remember your leaders, who spoke the word of God to you. And in the following verse 17: Have confidence in your leaders and submit to their authority, because they keep watch over you as those who must give an account. Do this so that their work will be a joy, not a burden, for that would be of no benefit to you. If, however, a preacher wants to honour this name, he must have God's mystery in a pure conscience and not preach to the souls entrusted to him weak words of human wisdom, but he should insist on the words of our Lord Jesus Christ and the doctrine of piety. 1 Timothy 6:3. He should preach this doctrine as a manifestation of the Spirit and of the power it has to move the hearts of the listeners. 1 Corinthians 2:4. He himself must, from his heart, be a model of the doctrine that he has submitted to, Romans 6:17, so that he does not become like those of whom Paul says Romans 2:20-23: an instructor of the foolish, a teacher of little children, because you have in the law the embodiment of knowledge and truth—you, then, who teach others, do you not teach yourself? You who preach against stealing, do you steal? You who say that people should not commit adultery, do you commit adultery? You who abhor idols, do you rob temples? You who boast in the law, do you dishonor God by breaking the law?

§ 19. In the fourteenth instance teachers and preachers are called servants of God as Paul calls himself with pride in the Holy Scriptures when he says that he was to be a minister of Christ Jesus to the Gentiles. He gave me the priestly duty of proclaiming the gospel of God, so that the Gentiles might become an offering acceptable to God, sanctified by the Holy Spirit. Therefore, I glory in Christ Jesus in my service to God. I will not venture to speak of anything except what Christ has accomplished through me in leading the Gentiles to obey God by what I have said and done. Romans 15:16-18. Therefore, he also says 1 Corinthians 3:5: What, after all, is Apollos? And what is Paul? Only servants, through whom you came to believe — as the Lord has assigned to each his task. And, in the following Chapter 4:1 he says:

This, then, is how you ought to regard us: as servants of Christ. Similarly, Colossians 1:7 Paul writes about Epaphras, that he is a dear fellow servant and a faithful minister of Christ. And he writes to his Timothy: If you point these things out to the brothers and sisters, you will be a good minister of Christ Jesus, nourished on the truths of the faith and of the good teaching that you have followed. 1 Timothy 4:6. Accordingly, even today every true teacher is a servant of Christ. But this means that he does not serve his stomach, nor the world, nor the will of carnal people, but he only serves Christ Jesus in his ministry and he should live in such a way that this, his Lord, can bring about everything in him that he has to teach others, so that he can carry out his ministry faithfully and serve God honestly.

§ 20. In the fifteenth instance the Holy Scriptures call faithful teachers and preachers co-workers of God as is said of the apostles 1 Corinthians 3:9: For we are co-workers in God's service; you are God's field, God's building. God works on the souls of men through certain mediators who he requires as assistants in the conversion of sinners. These mediators are the teachers and preachers, therefore they are called God's co-workers. Indeed, it is not as if God could not carry out his work on men without them, or it is not that conversion happens through teachers and preachers, but it is because the prescribed order of salvation demands this and God wanted, in this way, to counteract the weakness of men. But, in order that teachers and preachers do not carry this wonderful name in vain, they must be ardently united with God and, with the help of this union, they must have the same inclination as him for the conversion of men. In the strength they receive from him they should faithfully help him work in the world so that through their ministry many souls may be won. They should not worry if they themselves are consumed in the process, knowing that their work will be richly rewarded by God.

§ 21. In the sixteenth instance teachers and preachers are also called spiritual builders as Paul says 1 Corinthians 3:10-15. By the grace God has given me, I laid a foundation as a wise builder, and someone else is building on it. But each one should build with care. For no one can lay any foundation other than the one already laid, which is Jesus Christ. If anyone builds on this foundation using gold, silver, costly stones, wood, hay or straw, their work will be shown for what it is, because the Day will bring it to light. It will be revealed with fire, and the fire will test the quality of each person's work. If what has been built survives, the builder will receive a reward. If it is burned up, the builder will suffer loss but yet will be saved—even though only as one escaping through the flames. Those teachers, therefore, who want to be clever and wise builders like the holy apostle Paul should ensure that they do not erect a fragile wood-carving of reason based on worldly wisdom on the ground that has been laid or cover a flimsy wall with whitewash. Ezekiel 13:10. Rather, they should erect the structure of faith in their listeners through the pure and proven word of God in such a way that it can remain firm against all stormy winds and, in times to come, can survive the purification by fire.

§ 22. Finally, in the seventeenth instance teachers and preachers are called God's stewards in the Holy Scriptures as it says 1 Corinthians 4:1: This, then, is how you ought to regard us: as servants of Christ and as those entrusted with the mysteries God has revealed. And Titus 1:7 Paul says: Since an overseer manages God's household, he must be blameless. That is why Peter also says: Each of you should use whatever gift you have received to serve others, as faithful stewards of God's grace in its various forms. 1 Peter 4:10. The house that they must manage is the Christian Church, and the mysteries in it are the holy sacraments and the word of God with all the blessings of mercy that Christ has acquired for us. Teachers and preachers thus have to strive in earnest for the excellence that is required for the proper stewardship of God's congregation, so that they can preach God's word in an edifying manner and reveal the mysteries of divine advice to souls eager for salvation the way the holy Paul did, who writes Colossians 1:25-29 about himself: I have become its servant by the commission God gave me to present to you the word of God in its fullness — the mystery that has been kept hidden for ages and generations, but is now disclosed to the Lord's people. To them God has chosen to make known among the Gentiles the glorious riches of this mystery, which is Christ in you, the hope of glory. He is the one we proclaim, admonishing and teaching everyone with all wisdom, so that we may present everyone fully mature in Christ. To this end I strenuously contend with all the energy Christ so powerfully works in me.